Every instinct screamed at Egon to run. But he did not run. Reacting impulsively was what had gotten him into trouble in the first place. Egon closed his eyes for a moment. I will not pull out in front of the speeding car. I will not give them an excuse to come after me.

Instead of thinking, instead of yelling, instead of running, Egon focused on the unusual puffiness about Heinz's mouth, the narrow trickle of blood coming from his left eyebrow.

Egon flinched as another blow slammed into his friend's jaw. Another to the abdomen.

The men were laughing and joking again.

"Hey, you!" The voice was harsh.

Egon froze as he realized that the sound was directed at him.

Other Puffin Books
About World War II

Andi's War   Billi Rosen
Anna Is Still Here   Ida Vos
Between Two Worlds   Joan Lingard
The Devil in Vienna   Doris Orgel
The Devil's Arithmetic   Jane Yolen
Friedrich   Hans Peter Richter
Grace in the Wilderness   Aranka Siegal
Hide and Seek   Ida Vos
I Am a Star   Inge Auerbacher
I Was There   Hans Peter Richter
Lydia, Queen of Palestine   Uri Orlev
The Man from the Other Side   Uri Orlev
Mischling, Second Degree   Ilse Koehn
A Pocket Full of Seeds   Marilyn Sachs
Sheltering Rebecca   Mary Baylis-White
To Life   Ruth Minsky Sender
Touch Wood   Renée Roth-Hano
Transport 7-41-R   T. Degens
Tug of War   Joan Lingard
Twenty and Ten   Claire Huchet Bishop
Upon the Head of the Goat   Aranka Siegal

TO CROSS A LINE

by
Karen Ray

PUFFIN BOOKS

PUFFIN BOOKS

Published by the Penguin Group

Penguin Books USA Inc., 375 Hudson Street, New York, New York 10014, U.S.A.

Penguin Books Ltd, 27 Wrights Lane, London W8 5TZ, England

Penguin Books Australia Ltd, Ringwood, Victoria, Australia

Penguin Books Canada Ltd, 10 Alcorn Avenue, Toronto, Ontario, Canada M4V 3B2

Penguin Books (N.Z.) Ltd, 182-190 Wairau Road, Auckland 10, New Zealand

Penguin Books Ltd, Registered Offices: Harmondsworth, Middlesex, England

First published in the United States of America by Orchard Books, 1994
Reprinted by arrangement with Orchard Books
Published in Puffin Books, 1995

    5 7 9 10 8 6

LIBRARY OF CONGRESS CATALOGING-IN-PUBLICATION DATA
Ray, Karen.
To cross a line / by Karen Ray.
p. cm.
Summary: In 1938, after a minor traffic accident, seventeen-year-old
Egon Katz joins an increasing number of German Jews desperately
trying to find a way out of the country.
ISBN 0-14-037587-2
1. Jews—Germany—History—1933-1945—Juvenile fiction.
[1. Jews—Germany—History—1933-1945—Fiction.
2. Germany—History—1933-1945—Fiction]
I. Title.
PZ7.R2101325To 1995 [Fic]—dc20 95-19986 CIP AC

Printed in the United States of America

For EUGENE KATZ,
  who lived to
  tell his story,
  and for
JULIE GRUENEWALD KATZ,
  who did not.

1

Egon kissed the chocolate-covered cookie and slipped it into his shirt pocket, where it wouldn't get crushed.

He'd never given a girl a present before.

Of course it was only a Christmas cookie. Egon smiled to himself. And the girl was only Katarina Mueller, owner of the prettiest face in all of Germany.

Egon Katz pulled the ancient scooter into the alley. As he let the engine hiccup and sputter to life, he blew playful clouds into the frosty air. Once again he had survived the dark hours of the early morning, the flour in his lungs, the tedium of the baking, the heat of the ovens, and, worst of all, the shouted commands of the master baker.

For two hours Egon was free. Or as free as a seventeen-year-old got these days. For two hours the scooter was his. The bread was his. The world was his.

He didn't even have to think. It was as if the cycle knew its own delivery route and his hands automatically knew the standing orders. A dozen loaves of dark for the shoe factory, six dozen hard rolls for the sandwich shop, two dozen loaves of white for the hotel.

Egon had a good memory. He had done well in school. His mother had always told him to study hard so that he could go to college. His older brothers had gone—on scholarship—and Egon was smarter than they were. Everyone knew that.

No use complaining. Might as well cry over burned bread. Egon knew he was lucky. Nobody bothered him here. That was the main thing.

Quickly, Egon opened the compartment on the back of the old scooter and lifted an armload of the sturdy loaves, working-class bread. If he balanced it just so, he could manage the order in one load. If there was going to be time to talk with Katarina Mueller, he would have to work fast.

"Morning, Egon."

"Morning, Mrs. Schmidt."

There, he'd managed it in one go. Some of the proprietors just grunted at him, but no matter how busy she was— and at this hour of the morning she was very busy—Mrs. Schmidt always spoke to him. Most people were kind, Egon often reminded himself.

But then, most people in the city didn't know. That, too, was something Egon often reminded himself.

Three blocks ahead and a left at the double signal.

Two and a half years in the city and Egon still didn't know the names of all the streets. But he never got lost. He navigated the same way he did everything else, on instinct.

Six dozen rolls, and ten dozen pastries. Definitely two loads. With Christmas coming up, Mr. Jürgens had doubled his pastry order. Clearly there were still some people in a mood to celebrate.

"Morning, sir."

"Arrange the pastries on that platter."

Egon nodded. It wasn't his job, but what could you do?

"And Egon, starting next week I'll need two dozen additional pastries. The good ones, with the fruit filling."

"Yes, sir." Egon's hands flew over the platter.

"Should I send a note to your master?"

"I can take care of it."

"Fine. *Heil* Hitler."

"*Heil* Hitler." Egon sputtered the words, as he did every time. He should be used to it by now. The words didn't necessarily mean anything. They were all-purpose sounds, uttered in dozens of situations—greeting, dismissal, and exclamation point all in one. Dedot Jürgens wasn't any worse than the rest of them.

Sometimes Egon thought it was good that he had to say the words every day. Otherwise it might be easy to get complacent, to think he could just go on about his business and everything would be fine. The words helped him remember that everything was not fine.

As if he needed more reminders.

The Katzes were the only Jewish family in the village of Barntrup. Everyone there knew everything about everyone else. Town officials remembered that Egon's father, Max Katz, had served nobly in the army during the Great War. Neighbors remembered his freely shared knowledge of animal husbandry and his fairness in every transaction. Julie Katz was a gentle soul known to all as the talented and generous gardener of their small plot outside town. Egon was the youngest of eight children, nearly all of whom excelled at school.

When he was a young boy, the Katz family had been respected, if impoverished, members of the community. Within a few years, however, they were practically ostracized.

Egon remembered the roll call by religion at school, the rocks tossed his way, the name calling.

Later, three of his brothers and sisters had gone abroad

in search of better lives. Carl was in England. Herbert was in Brazil. And Sidonie—his oldest sister—was in America.

Worst of all was the way the police had acted when his sister Helene died.

Egon chewed his tongue.

Julie would slap him for thinking that way. His gentle, sweet mother. She had cried often, from the frustration of too many children and not enough food. And she had cried in arguments with Max over their children's future—Papa had wanted them in his animal business; Mama had wanted them educated. Yes, her tears were an all-too-common sight. Her anger, however, was reserved for only one subject: Helene.

His mother's favorite—they called her Leni—had always been a little slow, but she had the sweetest disposition. Egon had never met anyone as nice as Leni, and could she ever sew!

When their father died, a year and a half ago, Leni was the only one who could comfort their mother. And when the mourning period was over, when there were dozens of stones piled on the grave and it was time for them all to go back to their regular lives, Leni was the only one who had stayed home with their mother.

Julie was old now. She had been old for a long time. Even in Egon's baby picture she had white hair. She had had such a hard life. Someday Egon would make it up to her. He'd buy her a gold bracelet. Or a fancy house. Or he'd go to college—that's what she really wanted. He might not be able to right now, but someday, "when this madness was over," he would.

One day, two months after their father's funeral, Leni had simply disappeared.

4

The police officer was unconcerned. "An imbecile, wasn't she?"

"No!" It wasn't clear whether Julie's anger was due to the insult, or his use of the past tense. "Helene can read. She can cook. She sews beautifully and she has a job."

"An imbecile, that's what I've heard."

Egon's brother Bruno spoke up this time. "Leni manages quite well, but that's not the point. The point is that she's missing."

"A Jew imbecile." The policeman shook his head. "Maybe she fell into a ditch."

"Helene rides the bus every day. She is responsible. And she's lost."

"Responsible adults do not get lost."

"Maybe she was kidnapped."

"Do you have any evidence at all about what happened to your sister?"

"She left home at the normal time three days ago, but she never showed up for her job. She has not been seen since."

"Sounds to me like she drowned in a ditch."

"Then find me her body!" Julie was hysterical. "Let me hug her one last time. Let me bury her and mourn properly."

The rest of them looked on in helpless horror as Julie screamed and beat on the counter. "Help me! She has to be somewhere! People simply don't vanish."

That, however, was precisely what had happened to Leni, and there wasn't a blessed thing they could do about it. They had walked miles and miles, looking in ditches, along the railroad tracks, and everywhere else they could think of. As the months passed, the family, too, had come to speak of Leni in the past tense. All except Julie.

For as long as Egon could remember, she had ended every hopeful thought with "when this madness is over." After Leni disappeared, she never said it again. Madness had become the normal order of things.

In Barntrup maybe. It was easier here, in the city. You could get lost. And it wasn't so lonely. No one here identified him as "that Jew kid." In fact, most people thought him too good-looking to be Jewish. Still, it wasn't easy here either. Those Nuremberg Laws were ridiculous. Just because he was Jewish, he couldn't get a driver's license. Making deliveries was part of his job. What was he supposed to do?

Like everyone else, Egon simply broke the law (although he cleverly dodged that subject in his weekly letters home). He was careful, but still, it was risky.

Egon became even more discreet after that nasty business last month. In what had come to be called *Kristallnacht*, the "night of the broken glass," the government had organized systematic violence all over the country. Synagogues, businesses, and homes were destroyed. Men were arrested and taken into "protective custody." The windows of his mother's house were broken—so much for the kindly neighbors—and, worst of all, Egon's closest brother had been arrested. Bruno had spent a week in jail and was now trying to round up money to go to China. *China!* Might as well talk about going to Mars.

No, Egon clearly didn't need any *heil Hitler*s to remind him to watch his backside. Nineteen thirty-eight had been a bad year, but at least it was almost over. Thirty-nine was bound to be better.

But Egon didn't have to wait for the new year to be optimistic. The next stop was his last one. It was only seven-thirty. He could easily spend fifteen minutes at the Muellers'

6

coffee shop without being missed. Fifteen minutes alone with Katarina Mueller.

For the past several weeks Katarina had managed to be in the kitchen every day when Egon made his delivery. The first couple of times he thought it was a lucky accident, like the symmetry of her face was a lucky accident. But soon it became obvious that while their meeting might be lucky for both of them, it was no accident.

"How can you make all these pastries," she had asked one day, "and still stay so trim?"

"Oh, I never eat them." Egon had smiled. "I just deliver them to pretty girls all over town."

Every day he made her laugh at least once. Anticipating that laugh was what he thought about in the dark hours of the morning. Remembering it was what got him through the rest of the day, especially dreary, wet days like this one. He would need a really nice laugh, with her teeth showing just a little, to make it through today.

If only he could touch her.

Egon planned how he would pull the cookie out of his pocket, how he would tell a story about how he had made it specially for her, how he would hold it out to her in his open palm. That way she would have to touch him.

If only Egon could touch Katarina, it would get him through the whole week.

He never got the chance.

2

The rain had started just a few minutes earlier. It was like stones hitting Egon's face. He could feel the dampness coming through the seams of his cheap jacket and soaking his upper back, which caught the force of every frigid, miserable drop.

The intersection was busy and breaks in the traffic non-existent. Egon shifted in frustration, which sent an icy spoonful of water from his scarf down his chest.

The rain and the flat morning light challenged Egon's eyes.

Why was traffic always heavier in the rain? Where did all these people come from?

He felt so useless, standing there straddling the scooter, doing nothing except getting wetter by the moment. Worse than discomfort, however, was the fear of what would happen if he didn't get moving, and fast.

The compartment on the back of the scooter was not entirely waterproof. Oh, Herman Levi said it was, said that water only leaked in if Egon opened the door from the wrong angle. But Egon knew better. The compartment leaked. That was the simple truth of it. The thin, unfinished wood absorbed moisture for the first few minutes, but after that, the remaining bread and pastries would be ruined.

Egon watched the whizzing traffic, looking desperately for an opening, pissing away his few precious moments with Katarina.

The bread was getting ruined.

He was getting wetter and more frustrated by the moment.

There.

Egon merged, accelerating quickly.

Even more quickly he realized that he had misjudged the speed of the oncoming car.

It came at him like a rocket—a five-thousand-pound black rocket aimed directly for him.

His reflexes excellent, Egon struggled to maneuver the scooter out of danger. But it was hopeless. The same three wheels that made the cycle such a sturdy delivery vehicle also made it cumbersome. No match at all for a rocket.

As he hurtled through the air, Egon realized that even if he survived the accident, life as he knew it was over.

3

It was only a week since the accident, but it might as well have been a year. In that one week Egon lived through an entire year of emotions.

Spring: Maybe the police report will get lost. Maybe they will forget about the accident. No one was hurt, after all, and surely the government has more important things to worry about than a minor scooter accident.

Summer: They will forget. They will ignore me just as they have ignored me all along.

Autumn: The summons to court. So much for being left alone.

Winter: Which is worse? Driving without a license, or being in an accident with a Nazi businessman?

A year's worth of worry, all of it because he had hoped to save a few moments on a rainy morning . . . because he couldn't get a driver's license . . . because he was Jewish.

That simple fact of birth was apparently the only thing that mattered. So much for the peaceful existence he had cultivated. Once the authorities were aware of someone—him—they would never let up. Egon would be hounded, his job endangered, or worse. There was always worse.

* * *

EGON SAT IN THE HALLWAY outside the courtroom, uncomfortable in his one good set of clothes.

Otto Sprage, the man who had hit Egon, sat across the hall, clearly unconcerned. Egon had discovered that Mr. Sprage was a businessman and an enthusiastic member of the Nazi party. He owned several factories, and for him political activism was simply a part of doing business.

At least, that's what Egon suspected—what he hoped.

In their conversations, Mr. Sprage had always been polite to Egon. Fair.

Surely the judge would also be fair.

Egon hid his hands deep in his pockets. As long as his hands were in his pockets, he would be all right.

Otto Sprage quickly turned pages in his briefcase, making occasional notes. For him this whole business was just an annoying waste of time.

Egon ran his fingers over the seams in his pockets.

"Next."

Egon was so focused on his plight that he hardly noticed the official trappings of the courtroom—the dark, heavy furniture; the raised podium of the judge; the flags.

What he did notice was how quiet the place was. How alone he was.

The judge was a well-fed older man who didn't even look up as they entered. There was a stenographer and a court officer.

Otto Sprage sat at one table, Egon at the other.

As he sat on the hard wooden chair, Egon mentally rehearsed his story. Tone, he realized, was just as important as content. Every bone in Egon's body screamed to shout out both his own innocence and the general unfairness of the situation, or, better yet, to have it out with the man the way he had with the boys at school. But he couldn't do that.

The same instincts that helped him maneuver the complex city streets, the instincts that helped him blend in so well—those instincts now waved giant warning flags in his consciousness.

Egon's explanation had to be truthful, but vague. He needed to be soft-spoken, deferential. He had to admit his share of the guilt and point out Otto Sprage's speeding, while not looking like a finger pointer.

Egon planned to emphasize the pleasant fact that no one had been injured in order to deflect attention from his absent driver's license. He rehearsed phrases, calling special attention to the troublesome weather.

"Mr. Otto Sprage," the judge began, "please explain to us what happened on the morning of December third."

"Very well, sir."

Egon jammed his hands deeper into his pockets.

Otto Sprage began with information about his factories, his political affiliation, and his respected position in the community. "In fact, your honor," said Mr. Sprage, "I believe that our daughters attend the same boarding school."

The judge nodded and smiled.

They know each other.

"As for the incident in question, it was not yet full light and, as it had just started to rain, I was driving especially carefully.

"I was proceeding along Ober Street in the heart of Bremen at a modest rate when suddenly Mr. Katz pulled in front of me. I couldn't swerve to avoid him because of oncoming traffic. I jammed on the brakes, trying to stop but"—his hands turned upward—"it simply was not possible.

12

"Mr. Katz has stated his belief that we share the blame for the accident. If that were true, I would gladly own up to it, but quite frankly, any idiot"—he looked at Egon—"knows that drivers on the main thoroughfare have the right of way and that entering drivers need to wait until it is absolutely safe.

"Even more important"—he adjusted his tie—"it is my firm belief that fact-finding and apportioning of guilt is properly done not by the participants, but is, instead, the rightful province of the court."

"Absolutely," the judge said firmly. "And I don't need any help from a cheeky Jew boy."

Egon's fists threatened to tear through the linings of his pockets. He stared at the stenographer, who recorded every unpleasant syllable.

The judge turned to Egon as if in distaste. "What do you have to say for yourself?"

Egon's well-rehearsed speech had gone, vanished along with his hopes for fairness. He stood up and stammered a few sentences about his reliability, his exemplary school record, and his devotion to his work.

"Your master is a Jewish baker?"

"Yes, sir."

"You have no driver's license?"

"No, sir."

"You knew you were not allowed to drive?"

"With all due respect, sir, making deliveries is part of my job."

The judge motioned him to sit down and began writing in a large folder.

Egon's heart fell into his freshly polished shoes. That was it? Not one word about the accident?

Growing up as the youngest in such a large family, he

had always had plenty of company. A father to discipline and a mother to encourage. Brothers to advise and sisters to console. Egon had been on his own for two and a half years, but he had never really felt alone. Until now.

Still the judge wrote. Finally, without even looking up, he began to speak.

"In the name of the führer . . ." The judge stared at Egon. "Stand up."

Egon stood.

"In the name of the führer . . ." Again the judge glared. "Take your hands out of your pockets."

Reluctantly, Egon placed his hands at his sides.

"In the name of the führer, I pronounce you guilty. The fine is eighty marks, payable today."

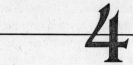

H ow can you possibly ask that?'' Herman Levi demanded.

Egon was direct but respectful, exactly as he had wanted to be in court. ''Sir, I was working for you, making deliveries at your direction, on your scooter. With all respect, it seems fair that we at least split the fine.''

''You stupid, thankless boy,'' Mr. Levi boomed. ''All this time we give you a good home, with plenty to eat. We teach you an honorable trade. And then you are careless enough to get into an accident—with a storm trooper, no less—and put us all in danger.

''Do I throw you out? Do I make you pay for the damage to the scooter? Do I punish you in any way?

''I do not,'' said Herman Levi, ''because I am a compassionate man. Inge, am I not a compassionate man?''

Inge Levi sat, folded into an embroidered throw pillow, wringing her hands as she always did at the slightest hint of trouble. She had been wringing her hands a great deal lately. ''Ach, Herman, of course you are a compassionate man.''

''When you started that fight with the journeyman, who paid for you to go to the doctor?''

Egon shifted uncomfortably in his chair. Once the master baker started in on a tirade, there was no point in responding. Egon had learned to simply endure the storm.

"Did I penalize you when you went home for your father's funeral? For taking time off to go to court? I did not, Egon, because I am a compassionate man."

Inge's hand wringing intensified.

"I know that it is hard to live in these times without a father. And that is why I have been so understanding. But Egon, you must learn to accept the consequences of your actions. Any father would want a son to learn that lesson. Someday I hope you will think of me as a father, and when that day comes you will be glad that I insisted that you clean up your own messes."

Egon shifted his weight, desperate to get away from the man. But if he moved before Mr. Levi was finished, there would simply be a lecture on manners along with the rest of it.

"Didn't you say the fine is due today?"

Egon nodded.

"Then you'd best get moving."

Alone in his closet of a room, Egon counted out his money. Eighty marks. An entire month's salary working at this miserable place.

If it were only himself, Egon would never have brought up the fine to Herman Levi. Egon didn't care about money. Not for himself. But with his brothers leaving the country, the money that Egon sent to his mother was all the more important. If he didn't send it, she would realize that something was terribly wrong.

Egon jammed the bills into his pockets. Somehow he would find a way to make up the eighty marks. He promised himself that no matter what happened, Julie would never find out about this.

5

As he left the bakery three days later, Egon cursed
every stroke of the creaky pedals. It was only
the second trip of the day.

The baskets on either side of the rear wheels and in front
of the handlebars made the bicycle difficult to balance and
awkward to steer. But bulky as they were, the baskets didn't
hold nearly as much as the compartment on the scooter. He
had to make at least three trips on the bicycle. Doing the
deliveries took more than twice as long as before. Barely
time for a quick wave at Katarina.

But the Muellers' coffee shop wasn't until the last load,
so he couldn't even look forward to that yet.

Egon braked at the busy intersection and stared at the
traffic. Even when the light turned green, he hesitated, making absolutely sure the opposing traffic had stopped.

He didn't need any more trouble.

Never had Egon been so aware of wanting to be anonymous. Before, blending in was something he did naturally,
like standing tall, or counting out change at the bakery.
Now, fitting in was something he worked at—like conjugat-
ing Latin verbs, or balancing an overloaded bicycle.

As he rode along the busy street, Egon was intensely
aware of every car that overtook him, of every pedestrian

whom he passed by. Was that man a party member? Was that woman Jewish?

Egon felt lucky that Katz was not readily identifiable as a Jewish name. What did it mean anyway, being Jewish? If being different in some way was important enough to be ostracized for, it ought to mean something. Not to Egon. He wasn't ashamed of it. He wouldn't deny it. But it had never done anything for him either.

Julie was religious. It was out of respect for her that their father never allowed pigs inside. And although they were too poor to even think about keeping kosher, Julie and his sisters would never eat pork. Often there was little enough food, and Egon had learned long ago not to be particular. Once, during his Hebrew lesson in the town next to Barntrup, Egon even asked the rabbi, if God felt so strongly about pork, why didn't he give them something, anything, else to eat?

Egon had gotten a rap across the knuckles for that. But the rabbi never did answer the question. After his bar mitzvah day Egon never went back to synagogue.

The bicycle was much lighter now. One more stop. Moses Weinstein's produce shop.

"Imagine that," Herman Levi had scoffed when the order came, "a *greengrocer* wanting to sell bread! And maybe I should start a cabbage stand."

"Some people live much closer to his shop than to yours," said an intrigued Egon. "It would be easier for them to buy bread *and* cabbages at one place. If you think about it, it makes sense."

" 'If I think about it'?" Herman Levi had erupted. "If I think about it. I think plenty! And I think that when people want bread they go to a baker, not a greengrocer."

Egon had kept his opinions to himself after that, but he

noticed that Moses Weinstein's order had increased steadily. Clearly people did buy bread from him, even if it cost a little more than at the bakery. Moses was a smart businessman. Used his brain. That's what Egon wanted to do.

Egon's father had called himself a businessman, too, but what a difference! Never enough food. Animals in the back room. Not enough water to wash with. Toilets that emptied into a gutter in front of the house. Everyone's houses in the village were just as primitive, but it was still disgusting—especially once Egon got to the city and saw how much better things could be.

Egon shuddered as he remembered holding the front legs of baby goats while his father sliced their throats. Egon was so small then, not much bigger than the animals. There were frantic cries and screams from the little goats as the knife went in. Suddenly, there would be silence. And then Egon's crying. His sensitivities irritated Papa, made him more determined to toughen Egon up. But no matter how much blood, offal, killing he saw, Egon never got used to it.

And then there was the incident that had revolted him more than any other. Papa had been selling a hog. Egon was weighing the pig in preparation for the sale. Buyer and seller were chatting amiably nearby. The nervous animal chose that particular moment to relieve itself.

"Egon"—his father had reacted instantly—"clean the pig shit off that scale!"

Egon had complied, though not so instantly.

Buyer and seller had continued their conversation. Max had smiled as he proudly called attention to Egon's actions. "No one will ever accuse Max Katz of trying to cheat a customer."

The humiliation and disgust of that moment was something Egon wouldn't ever forget, wouldn't ever let himself feel again.

"Morning, Egon."

"Morning, Mr. Weinstein."

Mr. Weinstein's shop was small and, like everyone else, he had a hard time getting inventory. Unlike everyone else, Moses Weinstein clearly worked hard to make the best of what he did get. Every head of cabbage was neatly trimmed. And there wasn't a speck of dirt clinging to any of the potatoes. Most of the produce shops had vegetables prepackaged in baskets, with bruised or rotten pieces carefully hidden at the bottom. Mr. Weinstein allowed customers to choose only the individual beets or carrots that they wanted.

And there, next to the vegetable scale, were the large baskets for the bread.

"Give me two of those, sonny." A dumpy woman grabbed the loaves directly from Egon's arms.

Moses smiled at him. "So what if Herman Levi thinks I'm crazy."

"You're not crazy, sir." Egon unloaded the remaining loaves into the baskets. Why couldn't Egon work for someone like Moses Weinstein?

Egon stared at the old grandmother overburdened with bulky shopping bags. Everywhere he went he saw them, the younger women burdened with children, the older ones with years of potatoes around their waists, trudging from shop to shop.

The idea had come to him several weeks ago, but he had been afraid to mention it. Now, though, a combination of exhaustion (anything to keep from getting back on that stupid bicycle) and financial need (anything to earn a few extra marks) gave Egon courage.

Purposefully Egon loitered while Mr. Weinstein listened

to the woman's tale of woe. To himself Egon went over and over what he would say. Of course, it would be more difficult with only the bicycle. Still, Egon was sure it was a good idea. It could work.

Finally the woman left.

"Is there something I can help you with, Egon?"

"Actually, Mr. Weinstein, I was thinking I might be able to help you."

"You have time, perhaps, to uncrate potatoes?" His laugh was not unkind.

"No, sir. I have a business proposition for you."

"You do? For me?"

"It's clear your customers appreciate the high quality and good service they get from you." Egon spoke quickly, before he lost his nerve. "Have you ever thought of offering a delivery service?"

Mr. Weinstein shook his head. "It's just me here, Egon. I couldn't do that and still mind the store."

"My idea"—Egon stopped and corrected himself—"my proposal is that *I* could become your delivery service." Now Egon really spoke fast. "I have a few hours off late in the afternoon. I would pay Herman Levi a small sum for the use of the bicycle. And I'm sure a great many of your customers would be willing to pay a small sum to have produce delivered right to their door."

Mr. Weinstein stared at Egon. "And what does Herman Levi think of this idea?"

Egon looked at the floor.

The man's voice was serious. "Would you like me to talk to him?"

"You'd do that?"

"Of course. Herman Levi already thinks I'm crazy. This will only confirm it." Now his laughter was conspiratorial.

"But if there's something in it for him, he'll be interested."
Mr. Weinstein stroked his beard. "His only possible objection would be that you might not have enough energy and slack off working for him."

"No, sir. Whatever I do, I always work hard."

"I'm sure you do, Egon." Mr. Weinstein paused for a long moment. "Your father's dead, isn't he?"

"Yes. I need the money to send to my mother."

"I'm sure we can convince Herman Levi to go along with the idea. Hard work is the best way I know to keep a young man out of trouble."

Egon shifted his weight uncomfortably. "Mr. Weinstein . . ."

"Yes?"

Trouble. The word ricocheted in his mind, reminding him of all the times at school he'd fought back with rocks or his fists. *Please, Egon, stay out of trouble.* They were his mother's parting words when he left home. For the hundredth time, Egon kicked himself for being in such a hurry that morning. It was his own fault—that was the worst of it. Much as he wanted to, he couldn't blame Otto Sprage or even the judge. But he could at least be honest about what had happened.

"The scooter did get hit, like I told you the other day." He paused. "I thought you ought to know that I had to appear for driving without a license and causing an accident. They made me pay a fine. Eighty marks. That's another reason I need the money."

Mr. Weinstein stared hard at him.

Egon's courage wilted. "I'll understand, sir, if you don't think this is such a good idea."

"Not at all." Mr. Weinstein put an arm around Egon's shoulder as they walked outside. "I do appreciate your telling me, though. A lot of people wouldn't have. Times are hard for all of us."

Egon got onto the bicycle.

"I'll chat with Herman later today. We'll talk more tomorrow." He extended his right hand.

Egon tried to confine his shaking to his hand. "You won't be sorry, sir."

Suddenly the bicycle was oiled with enthusiasm. The cold air felt cheerful on his face.

Had he told Mr. Weinstein about the fine because it was the right thing to do? Or because Herman Levi would have mentioned it anyway?

No matter.

Usually Egon rode methodically and was careful to avoid the numerous potholes. Now his feet twirled like dizzy hamsters. Every jolt threatened to throw his body up to join his already soaring spirits.

The few times he had ventured a suggestion at the bakery, both the idea and Egon himself had been roundly ridiculed. So he had stopped suggesting.

Moses Weinstein, however, listened to him and appreciated a new idea. Moses Weinstein offered to help him. Moses Weinstein even put himself and Egon in the same category. *Times are hard for all of us*.

Herman Levi, on the other hand, never allowed a hint of commonality between them. The man apparently thought the sun wouldn't set unless he reminded Egon at least twice each day who was the master and who wasn't.

Of course, it wasn't just making more deliveries that excited Egon. It was having a project all his own, having a little bit of independence. And what that independence could lead to. Before he was halfway to the bakery, Egon had saved to buy his own delivery bicycle. He had organized students all over the city in a centralized delivery service. He was president of his own company.

Egon might not be able to go to school, but no one would ever say he wasn't smart. And as long as he had legs to pump a bicycle, his mother would never go hungry.

Almost back to the bakery now. He was fairly bursting with excitement. Too bad he couldn't tell the Levis right away. Katarina—that's who he would tell. She would be happy for him. She would understand.

Egon clattered down the alley to the bakery and turned the bicycle around so that he would be able to fill the rear baskets quickly for the final load.

Inside the kitchen, he found Mrs. Levi, wringing her hands and pacing.

She saw him at the same moment.

"Ach, Egon, come inside. Come inside."

"I'm already in."

More wringing of hands. "Sit down, Egon."

"What's wrong?"

"I'm afraid Mr. Levi isn't here."

"So?"

She threatened to rub the skin off her hands.

"What happened, Mrs. Levi?"

"Oh, Egon. I'm so sorry. They came. They came for you."

6

W ho came for me?"

"I didn't know what to say, Egon." There were tears in her eyes. "I was so frightened. I've never spoken to one of them before."

"Spoken to *who*, Mrs. Levi?"

"Blackshirts. Two Blackshirts were here about fifteen minutes ago."

Egon froze.

The Brownshirts weren't always so bad. A lot of them were simply ordinary guys in soldiers' uniforms. Many were draftees. The Blackshirts were another story. Strictly volunteer, they were by far the most enthusiastic—and most cruel—soldiers in the whole German army. Even the name—Gestapo—gave Egon the creeps. He always crossed the street just to avoid walking near one of them. And now they wanted him.

Egon struggled to control his breathing, to keep his voice calm.

"What did you tell them, Mrs. Levi?"

"I said you were out making deliveries"—her voice cracked—"that there was no telling when you'd be back." She paused. "I told them you tend to be very irresponsible."

Thank God she had kept her wits. "And?"

"You are to report to Gestapo headquarters at six o'clock tomorrow morning."

Report. There?

"Egon," she whispered, as if even saying the words was a betrayal, "they had a warrant for your arrest."

Egon had foolishly allowed himself to believe that the ordeal in the courthouse was enough, that for eighty marks he could pretend the accident had never happened.

Instantly, his senses sprang to life.

Even now they might be watching the bakery, waiting for him to return.

He opened the door a crack and peeked into the alley Nothing.

Every moment he hesitated, however, was another opportunity for them to come back for him.

A second glance, and Egon went outside. He barely felt the weight of the bulky bicycle as he carried it into the kitchen.

"What are you doing?" Mrs. Levi whispered.

Egon glanced around quickly. There was no place to hide the bicycle. If he covered it up, that would only make it more obvious. He leaned it against the large worktable, then turned to lock the back door.

"Egon, what are you doing?"

"If they see the bicycle, they'll know I'm here." He hesitated. "This way they won't see it."

Egon climbed the narrow stairs that led to the Levis' living quarters. Mrs. Levi was right behind him.

He went up the narrower stairs to the attic and his modest room. Still, she was behind him.

Egon methodically began going through his belongings.

Mrs. Levi sat in the one straight chair. "What are you doing?"

For a moment they stared at each other. For some reason this absolute stillness was worse than her nervousness ever was. "I'm leaving."

"Now?"

"Yes." Carefully Egon appraised each pair of socks. Each shirt. Each handkerchief. He couldn't take everything. Cleaned-out drawers would be too obvious. Into his small satchel, Egon put a few pieces of clothing, his razor, the photograph of his parents, his letters, and the rest of his money. Fifteen marks. Frugal as he was, that wouldn't take him far.

On second thought, Egon replaced the razor. He moved quickly and efficiently, going through all the remaining possessions, making sure there were no stray clues.

Mrs. Levi sat, silent, watching his every move.

Packing complete, Egon sat on the bed. He shoved aside the stubby candlestick and used the nightstand for a desk.

Dear Mr. Levi,

    Unfortunately, circumstances require that I leave without being able to thank you personally for all you have taught me the past two and a half years. Perhaps someday

Suddenly Egon froze.

In one harsh movement he crumpled up the paper and jammed it into his pocket. He was a criminal now, or he would be in a few minutes. Any note he left would only put the Levis in danger. Better to have Herman Levi think him an ingrate than to bring the Blackshirts down on the Levis as well.

Egon looked over at Inge Levi.

Then he removed the note from his pocket and opened it.

Pffft. The candle match caught with only a slight hesitation. In a few flaming seconds the paper was reduced to ashes, which Egon carried carefully to the window.

One last time Egon studied the familiar items folded in his two drawers. No one looking at those drawers could tell that he never planned to return.

"Egon?"

He started at the unexpected sound. "Yes."

"When they return, what should I tell them?"

Egon hesitated only briefly.

"Tell them that I never came back. You've already told them I'm irresponsible. Harp on that. I'm sure Mr. Levi can be quite convincing about my shortcomings."

Another time they might have smiled at that.

Egon leaned over and rumpled the bedclothes. He wasn't the kind of apprentice who'd make the bed. He was a ruffian, a kid who simply took off, maybe to spend the day with some girl.

Mrs. Levi looked at him, then away. "You understand that I made up the part about you being irresponsible."

Please don't make this any worse.

She went on, "Mr. Levi isn't really so bad. This is just a very hard time for all of us. One of his brothers is still in prison from *Kristallnacht*, and there are all sorts of nasty rumors floating about. He's heard a rumor that early next year all Jewish businesses will be confiscated by the government. If that happens, I don't know how we'll live."

Egon refused to listen. He had troubles enough of his own. "If the bicycle is here, they'll know I was back. So I'll leave it around the corner in the alcove next to the shoemaker's. You know where I mean?"

She nodded.

"I'll put some trash in front, so it won't be so obvious. Probably best to wait until tomorrow to find it."

She nodded again.

One last glance at the room and Egon headed for the stairs. Halfway down he felt Mrs. Levi's hand in his.

It was a strange sensation. Neither one of the Levis had ever touched him. It was oddly pleasant, though, an acknowledgment that this wasn't easy for any of them.

Too soon they were back downstairs. The faint smell of baking lingered in the air. The room was still aclutter from their morning labors. Cleaning up was Egon's job.

Not anymore.

As he prepared to go out into the winter air, Egon buttoned his coat and pulled down his hat. As he reached for his gloves, Mrs. Levi stopped him.

She moved to shake his hand. Thinking better of it, she reached out to hug him.

"Good luck to you, Egon."

"Thank you. Thank you both for everything."

Gloves on, collar pulled up, Egon put his satchel in the front basket.

It might not be so bad. The satchel could be a book bag. He could simply be a boy on his way to school.

But it wasn't a book bag and he wasn't a schoolboy.

The first few minutes would probably be the worst. Egon unlocked the door and moved the bicycle into position.

"Egon?"

"Hmm?"

"Where will you go?"

He hesitated. "I don't know, Mrs. Levi. I really don't know."

7

Egon's cheeks were crimson. Not from the cold, but from the heat of his own body. Inside his coat Egon was damp. His hat itched his ears. His wool undershorts rode up uncomfortably.

As he maneuvered the bicycle outside, Egon looked around casually, as if checking for traffic. Nothing suspicious. The alley was deserted.

But what if he saw someone he knew? What if one of his friends asked why there wasn't any bread in the baskets? What if that busybody Mrs. Rosenfink stuck her nose in his face and asked straight out where he was going?

Those possibilities had not occurred to him before.

As he walked the bike, Egon quickly concocted a story.

An errand. An errand for Mrs. Levi. He was going to check on Mrs. Levi's mother, who was feeling poorly. Mrs. Levi couldn't go herself because she was expecting an important customer this morning.

And the satchel? That was mending Mrs. Levi had done for her mother. So sad . . . the poor old woman's eyes have been bad for some time. She's practically blind now.

Egon didn't want to use it, but having a cover story was better than not having one.

As he pushed his bicycle toward the end of the alley, he synchronized his breathing with his steps.

Right. Left. Inhale. Right. Left. Exhale.

Right. Left. Inhale. Right. Left. Exhale.

Only a few more steps to the corner now.

Right. Left. Inhale.

Around the corner, and there was the alcove. Egon kept his entire being focused on the next few minutes.

Right.

If he got caught now, hiding the bicycle, no one would buy a story about heading off to Granny's.

Left.

Working feverishly in the dim light, Egon balanced the bicycle, rearranged the rubbish, and moved on as if he were an ordinary boy headed off to school.

Exhale

8

Egon walked purposefully. It was morning rush, and he fit in easily with the flowing streams of coats, hats, and boots.

He chose, for now, to see his fellow pedestrians as items of clothing that moved. Far better that than bodies, faces that might try to make eye contact. People, all with hopes, fears, and dangers of their own.

Without hesitation Egon made his way along the familiar route. He'd come this way a dozen times.

There was a twinge at having lied to Mrs. Levi about where he would go. But what she didn't know, she couldn't tell. Now Egon was glad that he'd always been vague with the Levis about his extended family.

His cousins would be shocked, of course. But they wouldn't turn him away.

Samuel and Berta Katz had done well. Samuel owned a successful jewelry and crystal business.

"Wholesale is better," Samuel had reminded Egon more than once. "It's much less obvious than retail." Berta had a maid three days a week. *A maid*. They belonged to the best synagogue. They kept kosher. Their little girls, Hilda and Gudrun, were dressed like princesses. Best of all, they always treated Egon like family.

He was, of course. Still, he knew of many families where the struggling members were not always welcomed by the more successful ones.

He would have to remember that.

Since he'd been in the city, Egon had come for Passover and Shavuot and the other holidays. He'd come for birthdays and any other excuse.

This visit was clearly different.

For one thing, Egon was on foot. Even walking quickly, which he was, the journey would take him over an hour. Usually he would have taken the trolley. Not today. Partly it was the money. Never in his life had Egon been so aware of the need to save every pfennig.

Safety, however, was an even more pressing concern. Police officers randomly patrolled all public transportation now. For the safety of the passengers.

Surely they wouldn't be actively looking for him. Yet.

Still, Egon had no desire to come under even casual scrutiny. Nor to be confined in a streetcar with dozens of other people. And walking was good—something to keep his mind occupied.

He was concerned. He was extremely concerned. But at this moment Egon wasn't really afraid.

Samuel and Berta would tell him what to do. Whatever needed to be done, he would do. He could lie low for a while. He could go stay with Bruno in Hamburg. Or he could leave the country. Eventually, he was sure, it would come to that.

Carl and Herbert had left. Sidonie had left.

But they were adults with educations and jobs. He was a baker's apprentice with fifteen marks and an arrest warrant.

It was a crushing truth. Although Egon told himself that Berta and Sam would help him—*surely Berta and Sam would help*—with every block the starkness of his predicament became more and more clear.

He had no job. No money. No home. Even if he got the money, he couldn't leave the country because he had no passport. He couldn't get a passport. And if the police got him . . .

That was a possibility he refused to consider.

Right. Left. Inhale.

There was less traffic now. He was out of the city center. The workers were mostly in their offices, the children in their classrooms.

Hard to believe that earlier this morning he was going into business with Moses Weinstein. Two hours ago he was more optimistic than he had been in months. Now this.

What would Mr. Weinstein think when Egon didn't show up tomorrow? Egon didn't care about Herman Levi, but Mr. Weinstein had believed in him. Would he now believe the worst?

Egon tightened the buckle on the satchel. It wasn't heavy, but the rhythm of the bouncing against his back was annoying.

Times are hard for all of us.

It was reassurance enough.

Only six more blocks now. Egon was entering the well-to-do Jewish section. Here was a kosher butcher. There a Hebrew day school. And there, in front of the park, the sign had been defaced with a swastika.

Egon looked away.

Five blocks. Now four.

Fortunately, this morning he had not seen a single policeman or soldier—black shirt or brown. That was unusual. They were everywhere now, as much a part of life as the dreary weather.

34

But not today. Maybe it was an omen. Maybe everything would be all right for him.

Three blocks. Two.

With every step he began to relax a little. Today he would be able to play silly games with little Gudrun and Hilda. Today he would be able to sit on his cousins' velvet furniture, drink from their crystal glasses. Today they would help him out of this predicament.

Today.

9

As Egon waited for Berta to answer the door, he stared at the mezuzah on the door frame. It was made of polished brass, with curlicues of ornamentation and a tiny window through which Hebrew letters were visible.

Like all the trappings of religion, it left him ambivalent or, if he stopped to think, full of questions. Why those particular Bible verses? Why the right side of the door frame? Not horizontal, not vertical, but diagonal. Why did it matter?

And most important, why was Berta taking so long?

"Egon, what are you doing here?"

He stood there gaping at Berta's familiar face. He wanted to hug her. He wanted to be hugged. To be reassured. The last thing he wanted to do was talk.

Berta stared, shock and puzzlement dancing across her face.

Finally she came to her senses. "Sorry, Egon. Come in. Come in."

Still she stared at him, and still he couldn't say anything.

Finally he got the embrace he craved. And there, close to him, he felt warmth and acceptance. Perhaps even love.

Over Berta's shoulder Egon stared into the formal living

room. He studied the elaborate tasseled curtains, the menorah on the mantel, the large photograph—with silver frame—of Sam and Berta and the girls. There were lace doilies on the arms of the chairs and real wildflowers pressed into the lampshades. If a Jewish family could live this way, surely there was hope.

"Would you like some coffee?"

Egon nodded.

Usually there would be jokes about whether the coffee was real or some chicory substitute. No jokes today.

Egon focused on Berta's hands as she worked. He studied, as if it were the most important thing in the world, how fluidly she scooped and poured. Her hands were small, efficient. At just the right moment they reached for the cups and spoons. Normally—if he could imagine a normally—she and he would stay and drink their coffee in the kitchen. Now, though, her hands placed everything on a tray and led the way back to the living room.

As Egon stirred milk into his coffee, the spoon handle became hot to the touch. Sterling silver.

"I didn't know what to do, Berta."

Her hands were patient.

"While I was out making deliveries this morning, two Blackshirts showed up at the bakery with a warrant for my arrest." Egon sought to match Berta's composure with his own, telling the story slowly and methodically, as if it had happened to someone else. He didn't bother to tell her how terrified he was. Surely she knew that. Instead he concentrated on the details and the practicalities.

"I didn't know where else to go," he said finally. "So I came here."

Her hands were still.

Egon took a large drink of the coffee, wanting it to burn

the inside of his mouth so that he would have something else to think about. "I hope it's all right that I came."

"Certainly, Egon. I was just thinking."

"I don't want to get you into trouble, too."

Her hands waved the idea away. "Let me telephone Samuel."

Egon still thought of the telephone as a novelty for rich people. But as he watched Berta's hands operate the black machine, it occurred to him that a telephone might be a convenient device.

"Frieda, this is Mrs. Katz. May I please speak to Mr. Katz."

She listened, then hesitated briefly. "Tell him it will only take a moment."

Berta looked up and smiled at Egon as she waited for her husband. "Sorry to disturb your meeting, Sam, but the oven just blew up."

She waited as he asked a question.

"There's no fire"—her voice was calm—"but I'm quite sure it's the oven."

Egon gaped. How could they possibly talk about kitchen problems at a time like this?

"I'll need to call for repairs," said Berta, "maybe even a whole new oven. But with all the expenses recently, I knew you'd want to be informed." And she hung up the receiver.

Not one word about him. Egon was wrong about the telephone. Clearly it was not just a toy for rich people. It was a toy that caused them to go soft in the head.

"Sam will be here in a few minutes."

Egon squeezed his coffee cup. "Sorry to hear about your oven."

"That was code, Egon. You're the oven."

10

I thought it was you and the girls," whispered Sam. He hugged Berta fiercely.

Egon stood by, embarrassed. He'd never seen his parents touch this way. The greater source of discomfort, though, was the realization of just how disruptive his presence—and his situation—actually was. It was one thing for Egon to run away in a panic. It was quite another to see Sam and Berta's instant grasp of his predicament.

"We have to get you out of the country," said Sam. "I don't see any way around that."

Egon nodded, somewhat reassured by Sam's use of the word *we*.

"I've got some ideas," Sam went on. "I'll go out in a few minutes and talk to a couple of friends. But I'm not going to mislead you, Egon. Getting you out right now is not going to be easy—or safe."

"Will it be more dangerous than reporting to Gestapo headquarters tomorrow morning?"

They sat, silent, on the couch across from him.

Egon stared back at them. His voice was flat. "I didn't think so."

"I'm glad you understand the seriousness of what's going on here." Sam squeezed Berta's hand. "So many people just want to believe that one way or another everything will turn out all right. Those people are wrong. And if you recognize the seriousness of the situation, as you obviously do, it will give you courage to do what needs to be done." Sam stood up to leave. "Egon, I hope you can understand why I don't want Hilda and Gudrun to know that you're here."

Egon chewed the inside of his cheek as he nodded. Would he never see any of them again? Never hear Hilda's incessant questions? Never feel Gudrun's plump cheeks and arms as she gave him a hug?

He listened as Sam and Berta discussed how to manage the midday meal. Normally, of course, the girls came home and they ate the main meal of the day together.

"I could ask Leah Reichmann to give the girls dinner," Berta said.

"Good idea," Sam said cheerfully. "Remember you've had quite a difficult morning with the kitchen. I'm sure she'll understand."

As Sam headed for the door, he turned back. "Don't want you two to get bored while I'm gone. Maybe you could rig up some sort of oven disaster." He smiled. "Nothing too elaborate, but let's make sure the smell is such that any surprise visitors won't want to stay long."

As SHE GOT OUT MIXING BOWLS, measuring cups, and baking ingredients, Berta kept up a steady stream of chatter. They had gotten a letter from Sidonie in America. Hilda and Gudrun were growing out of their clothes. The weather seemed a little mild for December. Perhaps it would be an easy winter.

Cheering up that didn't.

Egon squatted in front of the gleaming oven. The handle

was polished wood and there was a dial in the center that read the temperature inside. The door opened smoothly and there was insulation to keep the heat in. There was a rack that could be raised and lowered. The oven was large enough to hold not just a roast goose, but an entire goose dinner. What Julie wouldn't give for an oven like this. Such a pity to ruin it.

". . . so then Hilda said, 'I may not be much bigger than her, but I'm still Gudrun's *big* sister.' "

Egon surveyed the implements and the ingredients on the table. Everything was top quality. The eggs were clean. No weevils in the flour, no sour smell emanating from the butter bowl.

The stirring spoon felt heavy in his hand. Not only silver—he glanced at his reflection in the spoon—but recently polished silver at that.

Every speck of his training, both at the hands of Herman Levi and, earlier, from Julie, said to respect such quality. In these times, quality was a rare and valuable thing. Yet every speck of his being urged him to have his fun wherever he could find it. In these times, fun was a rare and valuable thing.

He would imagine it was Julie's rickety oven he was doing in, that afterward he would call—on the telephone, of course!—and order her a new one with a polished wood handle and superb insulation. Perhaps with silver knobs and a set of spoons to match. Never again would she have to cart her holiday *butterkuchen* to the village baker for cooking because her oven was so inferior.

It would be easy, and rewarding, to get rid of Julie's troubles for her.

Egon rubbed his hands together. "We'll need to get the oven very hot."

Berta cranked it up.

"Say you used too many eggs, or too much leavening."

"You're the expert." Berta nodded conspiratorially.

Egon held his hand high above the bowl and poured theatrically. No need to measure. "If that doesn't do the trick, we can plug the vents. That would tune things up."

"I never did like to cook. This is going to be a wonderful excuse."

Pssss. Egon slopped batter onto the sides and floor of the oven. He left two half-filled cake pans inside for effect.

For several moments the two of them stared at the oven door. Inside there was sizzling and popping.

"That should do it," he said.

"Remember, Egon," she teased, "I don't want to have to cook for at least a week."

"I used lots of extra butter. It'll burn easily."

Silently Egon and Berta put away the flour and sugar, the salt, the eggs, and the little remaining butter. Behind them the smoke at first eased out around the oven door. Quickly it gathered momentum and the puffs became fierce clouds.

Berta waved Egon away from the sink as she washed out the mixing bowls and spoons.

Egon stood near his cousin, watching her purposeful, strong hands. Every instinct told Egon to turn around, shut off the oven, and open the windows. Instead, he simply stood there. The increasingly dark smoke clouded the air and assaulted his nostrils. No matter what happened, Egon knew he would smell that smoke as long as he lived.

11

There are three options."

Egon nodded. *Three*. That was encouraging.

Sam toyed with a piece of cheese. "It's your life, Egon. And you need to be the one to make the decision."

Egon, Sam, and Berta sat at the kitchen table. The supper Berta had prepared stiffened in the serving dishes. Their tenuous appetites had not been improved by the lingering smoke.

Egon had never listened so hard in his life. Sam and Berta would help him, he had known they would. Now that the time had come, however, he found that his reaction to that help was not the simple relief he had expected. He was reassured, certainly, by their support. But he continued to be terrified by the need for it. A part of him kept waiting for his fears to be dismissed as hysterical—*"Don't worry, Egon, everything will be fine"*—but instead his fears had not been dismissed, only confirmed. It was one thing for a seventeen-year-old baker's apprentice to run away in fright. It was quite another for a respected businessman seriously to advise sneaking out of the country.

"First thing," said Sam, "is that you shouldn't make any decision based on money. Berta and I will help you."

"Thank you. And someday I'll repay you."

"Not us." Sam shook his head. "When you are able, you should help out someone else."

Egon nodded.

"As I said, without a passport you have three choices.

"First, a ship leaves tomorrow for South America." He looked at his notes—"Paraguay"—then back to Egon. "A number of Jews are going to South America. As far as we know, they are being left alone. That would also put you close to Herbert."

"He's in Brazil."

Sam shrugged as if it were an inconsequential difference.

"But there is one major drawback." Sam broke eye contact. "The ship requires all males over fifteen to have an affidavit that shows they are exempt from the German draft."

"So much for that. What's the second choice?"

"Sweden. There are no affidavits. No controls. Ships leave four days a week. And it's not so far away."

Sweden sounded far away. "And the third choice?"

"A friend of a friend is smuggling Jews across the Dutch border by passing them as miners."

Egon examined the idea in his head. "I've heard they don't bother Jews in Holland."

"I've heard the same thing." Sam's voice was even.

"What about China?" Berta spoke up. "We've been hearing about the new Jewish relief organization there."

Sam shook his head. "It takes weeks to arrange passage."

Egon had been too preoccupied to notice before that for Sam and Berta this was obviously familiar ground. "Are you going to China?"

"It's very complicated for us, Egon . . . the girls, the business. . . . We're not sure of anything right now."

Egon nodded. "The baker's wife told me the government isn't going to allow Jews to have businesses."

Sam's fist clenched. "Who knows what nastiness is in store?" His voice softened. "For now, let's get you safe."

Egon crumbled a piece of bread onto his plate. "The German army definitely doesn't want me, but I'm afraid they're not going to help me leave. That eliminates the first one." He stared at Sam. "I don't know a word of Swedish. And there aren't any Jews in Sweden, are there?"

"Maybe not Jews." Berta spoke softly. "Surely there are bakers."

Holland. Egon said the name in his mind. It was close. The language wasn't as much of a problem. Being Jewish wasn't as much of a problem.

"Have you got a pickax?" Egon's voice hadn't cracked in a long time. "I've always wanted to be a coal miner."

12

Alone in the attic, Egon thought about everything but the task before him.

He listened to the happy laughter of the girls downstairs. Apparently the oven disaster—he could smell it even up here—was the source of much teasing, which Berta bore with great good humor.

For the dozenth time he reread the address on the small slip of paper. Again he picked up his coat and was reassured by the stiff places at the hem: money that would help him buy his freedom. He did not look at the writing paper on the cot.

It was surprisingly warm, almost uncomfortably warm, up here.

Dust was everywhere. Every time he moved, little clouds rose up. There was a heavy layer of it on the small window. His hands were filthy with dust. It danced in the air and almost certainly seeped through the tea towel Berta had placed over his food. He wasn't hungry anyway.

The sounds from below were winding down. Hilda and Gudrun were getting ready for bed. Usually he would be doing the same. Two and a half years of getting up at two-thirty had taught him the wisdom of going to bed early.

Not tonight. Egon doubted whether he would be able to sleep at all. At five o'clock Sam would take him to the train station. So there would be plenty of time yet to write the letter.

What could he tell her anyway?

"Tell Julie whatever you like," Sam had said. "We'll keep the letter for you. Then, when we know you're safe we'll make sure it gets to her."

Sensible. Like all of Sam's advice. Soon, though, Egon would be all alone, without a syllable of advice. Without a shoulder to turn toward. Without a face he could trust.

Would he ever see his brothers and sisters again? Sidonie, Carl, Herbert, and, of course, Leni, were all gone. There was Gertrud, whose little girl, Susan, always greeted him with such a smile. Cecilie was soon to be married. And Bruno, his closest brother and friend, taught school in Hamburg.

Egon couldn't tell his mother how he felt at the thought of never seeing her again. He was her youngest child and her greatest hope. She had had a little more time when he was little and had used it wisely, filling his ears with tales of a better life. There were exhortations on staying out of trouble and there was advice on studying hard. "Whatever's in here"—she would rap him on the head—"nobody can take that away from you."

The more Egon thought, the more impossible the task seemed. Sam had said they would get her the letter after he was safe. But there was the real possibility that he would not be safe. He could be sent to prison. Or killed.

Julie would get his letter no matter what. She would put it under her pillow, search between the words for clues, wear the paper out with her eyes.

Egon filled and emptied the pen several times.

Dear Mama,

So many important things to say. So little time and so few words. My strength has always been quick thinking, not deep thinking. So if I stumble here on paper—if I can't articulate all the things that need writing—don't worry about me. I'm applying that quick thinking where it's most needed.

I know that many times when we were small you cried because we had so little. But we had something more important than fancy clothes or rich meals. We had a mother who taught us well. Because of you I have the strength to do what needs to be done.

Thank you for that and for everything.

Love, your son Egon

13

Darkness had never been so dark. Stillness had never been so still.

It was the early hours of the morning and Egon sat on the cot, his head and upper body propped against the wall, his legs extended under blankets.

What would it feel like to be shot?

At least if he were shot, it would be over quickly. Dying might not be so bad. Better than being beaten up and left to rot in some prison.

A sound.

Instantly Egon sat up straighter. His eyes opened wider.

There it was again, the scraping sound.

Someone was downstairs. Egon stiffened involuntarily. It had not occurred to him that they might come for him here.

Feet were on the stairs.

Too dark to search out a hiding place

Step. Step.

He held his breath as the door opened.

"Egon?"

"Yes." Egon's heart drummed against his ribs.

"I couldn't sleep either." Sam kept his voice low. "Would you like some company?"

"Sure."

Sam sat down on the foot of the cot. "You made the right choice, Egon, the same choice I would make. The people are supposed to be trustworthy. You are definitely young and strong." He paused. "A good coal miner."

"Then why can't either one of us sleep?"

Sam reached for Egon's hand. "These are scary times. One of the reasons I couldn't sleep is that I kept wishing I was you."

"What?" Nothing could have shocked Egon more. "How could you possibly wish that?"

"Because you're leaving," Sam said simply. "Because you are seventeen years old, and in a few days, for you, this will all be just a bad memory."

"But you're leaving too." Egon was careful to make it a statement, not a question.

"Yes. We're leaving. But we have to get priority numbers, passports, sponsorships, health certificates. All of that calls attention. What if the government stops emigration? You get to leave now. Better ten months too early than ten seconds too late."

Egon was discomfited. He didn't want to be pitied, but neither did he want to be envied. He wanted to change the subject. "I hope that helping me doesn't make things difficult for you."

"Not to worry yourself." Sam waved the thought away. "I'm just glad it was the maid's day off."

"But she's Jewish, isn't she?"

"Of course. It's just that . . . it's sometimes hard to know how a person will react in a stressful situation.

"You have good instincts, Egon. Be careful who you trust."

As Sam returned downstairs, it occurred to Egon that

soon the only person he would truly be able to trust was himself.

LIKE THE POLITE HOUSEGUEST HE WAS, Egon rose well before the appointed hour. He left the blankets neatly folded on the cot and gave his sleeping quarters one last glance before moving down the stairs, gently, so as not to disturb sleeping members of the family.

Yes, his mother had taught him well.

"Morning," Berta whispered as he entered the kitchen. "Did you sleep?"

"Some."

"Anticipating is always the worst part. Once you're on your way, everything will be fine."

Sam was silent, sipping coffee. Did he agree?

"I packed a snack that should fit in your satchel."

Egon unbuckled, inserted the packet, and rebuckled. As long as he didn't have to talk very much, he thought he would be all right. If he actually started to . . . No . . . Egon's throat seized up. He bit the inside of his cheek instead.

"Is there anything else you need?" Sam asked.

Egon shook his head. "The razor was it."

Sam held his hand against Egon's cheek. "We can't have you looking like a hooligan."

Berta looked at Sam. "Are you sure we shouldn't try to round up some work boots, or sturdier clothes?"

"And perhaps he needs a pickax and a bucket for the train ride?" said Sam. "No. There's enough sewn into the coat for Mr. Ritter to get him whatever he needs."

"If you're sure." Berta set boiled eggs and hard rolls in front of them.

Egon put the napkin in his lap. Politeness again. His

fingers unshelled, his spoon scooped, and his jaws moved. The food, however, might as well have been made of wood. Egon ate because it was a task before him, something that would help him get from this minute to the next one.

Spoons clicked, coffee poured, and food disappeared, all without aid of conversation.

Finally Sam cleared his throat. "All right, son, it's about time to leave. We don't want to miss that train."

Egon made a quick pass at his mouth. "I'm ready." The surprising thing was that he was. No more thinking. No more worrying. Another minute and he would be *doing*.

Address in pants pocket. Coat with slight thickness at the hem. Hat. Gloves. Satchel.

Hug.

Berta's arms were tight around him. His were tight around her.

. . . As long as he didn't have to look at the tears in her eyes.

He and Sam headed for the back door.

"Be careful, Egon. Please be careful."

I will.

It was still black outside and much colder than he had expected. As they started down the steps, Egon clenched his arms against his sides for warmth.

One last reminder from Julie. Egon turned around. "Shalom."

The tears graced Berta's cheeks now. "Shalom, Egon."

14

The train headed south.

No commuters were leaving the city this morning. Instead the dull cars were less than half filled with families and still-sleeping children headed somewhere for an early Christmas holiday.

It was Wednesday, December fourteenth. Only eleven days since the accident. Hard to believe that everything could change so much in so short a time. Egon felt as if his life had been severed by one of his father's whetted cleavers.

On the left was his life before the accident. On the right was his life after. On the left, the known and familiar. Family. Job. Getting up early and working hard. His little room at the Levis'. And on the right was . . . what? Fear, and terrifying uncertainty. But if he was honest, there was also excitement. For over two years he had hated being a baker's apprentice. Now he was no longer a baker's apprentice. Tomorrow he wouldn't even be in Germany.

Egon stifled a smile. No one else was smiling at this hour of the morning.

Syke. The last stop before the long ride to Diepholz and on to Osnabrück, where he'd change trains. Finally the sky was starting to lighten. Six o'clock. His appointed hour with the secret police.

Were the Blackshirts even now hammering on the bakery door? Was Herman Levi cursing the day he met Egon? Was the master baker himself making the deliveries on bicycle? Again Egon stifled a smile.

What would Katarina think when he didn't show up this morning? And Moses Weinstein? Was Egon's name even now clattering over the telegraph to be added to the list of troublemakers every policeman carried in his pocket?

No more thoughts of smiling.

After the first of the year every man, woman, and child in Germany would have to start carrying identification papers at all times. Jews would be clearly and officially identified. Every girl and woman would have "Sara" added to her name. Every boy and man would have an added "Israel."

Egon Israel Katz.

He recoiled at the very thought, amazed that until a few days ago he had accepted the idea, along with the rest of their garbage.

Eleven days' worth of frustration, eleven years' worth of anger, erupted silently inside of him.

So what if he had pulled out too soon? It was a dented-up scooter, that's all it was. If he were Christian, no one would care. Why was he running for his life? The crime and punishment were so out of proportion it made no sense. A teacher might as well have said that four plus four equaled not eight, but eight thousand. Suddenly. That's just the way it was, and you damn well better remember it.

Restrictions that had been part of the wallpaper of life thrust themselves before him as fresh insults. Why couldn't he have a driver's license? Why couldn't he go to college? One thought punched into the next. How could the world suddenly go insane the way it had on *Kristallnacht*? Why was dating a German girl a "disgrace against the race," a crime of Dachau proportions? Why did the drawings of Jews in the newspaper look so different from anyone he knew, almost like animals? Why didn't anyone care about Leni? How was Julie going to eat?

Why didn't someone *do* something?

Sara. Israel.

How would Otto Sprage and that damn judge like it if they had to carry around papers with something extra thrown into their names? What if one day the party decided that red was no longer red but green? Would that make it so?

Egon pulled at a thread in the upholstery next to him. He allowed himself a tight smile of satisfaction as the thread pulled free. Using small movements and his body as a shield, he worked at the area, doing his best to undermine the tight stitching. It was little enough.

He was not going to be Egon Israel Katz. Instead, he was going to be a coal miner. A free coal miner.

On the off chance he was stopped, he would not be expected to have identification papers, not before the first of the year. He was a schoolboy on holiday. A Christian schoolboy going home for Christmas. And tomorrow he would be free. The more he thought about it, the happier he was to be leaving Germany.

"Tickets. Tickets."

The bored conductor punched Egon's ticket.

He tried to ignore the swastika on the man's upper arm. Everyone in any sort of official capacity wore one now. They had even slipped one onto Egon's arm that day he worked at the motorcycle races. In his mind, Egon did what he had been afraid to do in fact. He ripped the offending symbol from his arm, spitting on it the way he had been spit on.

"Mama, I want some chocolate."

On the bench across the aisle, the mother ignored her little boy.

"Mama, I want some chocolate. *Mama, I want some—*"

"And I want a raspberry tart," she snapped. "There's no chocolate and there's no raspberry tart, so will you please shut up. Here." She shoved a small toy truck at him.

The boy made engine sounds as he scooted the truck back and forth across the nubby upholstery.

Everyone was awake now. Newspapers and books were out. Noses were pressed against the dirty glass, staring at the dreary landscape.

This was a good car, relatively new. Other than the small area beneath Egon's right thigh, there were no apparent flaws in the upholstery. The heater obviously worked—he wedged his coat between his body and the wall—and the car even had a reasonably good suspension system. The motion was not the sharp jolting he had expected from previous rides. Instead, the train's rocking motion was almost soothing. If only he had a newspaper, or something—anything—to do.

The boy across the aisle was whining again. This time the mother produced some tiny candies—not chocolate—and when they didn't inspire the desired silence, she whispered angrily into the boy's ear and swatted him across the bottom. No silence then either.

How Egon would have appreciated a truck like that. Or sweets of any kind.

The little boy looked about four years old and, despite the present behavior, was probably easily entertained. Egon remembered the nursery songs and finger games his mother had used instead of trucks and candies. Egon himself had used them with great effect with his only niece, Susan.

Egon rehearsed the rhymes in his head, planning out silly movements to accompany the even sillier songs.

He made eye contact and waved at the little boy, who hesitated a moment, then waved back.

Suddenly, however, Egon thought better of the idea. Who knew in what dangerous directions conversation with a stranger might lead. And even if Egon could—as he was sure he could—successfully deflect unwelcome questions, playing with the boy would call unnecessary attention to himself.

"Of course I remember him." Egon could imagine the woman's voice.

"He seemed so nice—singing with my son on the train. You never can tell, though, can you? And now that you mention it, there was something about him. He sat on his coat. And he looked suspicious. Obviously Jewish."

It was far better to remain a part of the furniture.

The boy waved again.

Egon looked away. Hands deep in his pockets, Egon fingered the small slip of paper. He didn't even need it; he'd memorized the address as Sam wrote it down for him. Egon realized, in fact, that he should destroy the paper. But he couldn't do that. This little slip of paper—the size of his thumb—was the only tangible connection he had with his new life. His free life.

No.

Egon recognized him as surely and instantly as a mouse identifies a hawk.

A Blackshirt.

He meandered into the car, glancing about for an empty seat.

Dear God, please not next to me.

The man looked to be about thirty. He was square and polished. His pistol rode easily on his waist.

Instantly Egon wished that he'd selected a less desirable car, that he'd set his coat on the seat beside him.

The man was three rows away. Now two.

"That seat taken?"

Seemingly on its own, Egon's chin swung side to side.

The black presence was next to him now, so close their pants were almost touching. With great determination, Egon resisted the urge to get up and visit the toilet, to find a car with no heat and torn seats, to jump off the train.

Instead he half closed his eyes, feigning that sleepy-bored expression of long-distance travelers everywhere.

If I can't manage this, how am I possibly going to do as a miner waltzing across the border?

The train, which had been going at quite a clip, now seemed painfully slow. Egon mentally encouraged the boy across the aisle to whine and cry, have a tantrum over toy trucks, chocolate candies, and nursery songs.

It wasn't going to happen. A quick glance told Egon that the rascal had turned into an angel, now curled up asleep in his mother's arms.

The hole in his seat. The hole he had torn in the upholstery suddenly assumed gaping proportions. Surely the spot was hidden by his legs—he glanced down to be sure—but what if the man had some other method of detection? Were there upholstery threads beneath his fingernails? No. Was there a guilty look on his face? Egon wanted very much to avoid that question. But it was unavoidable, like the man sitting next to him, the hole underneath him, the uncertainties ahead of him. He might not look Jewish, but looking guilty would be just as bad.

Egon leaned his head into the window. One by one he

focused on his features. Forehead. Eyes. Mouth. He aimed not for a particular expression, but absolute blankness, a lack of expression. Sleep, at this hour, might be obviously odd, so he kept his eyes open, allowing them to take in everything, but without staring.

Cheeks. Relax.

Ears. Not much to be done with them.

Tongue. Relax, stop pressing on his teeth.

Hands were the hardest. His pockets beckoned, but he didn't want to appear as if he had anything to hide. Instead, he concocted an elaborate casualness, one hand resting atop the other, fingers draped just so.

When finally convinced of his own innocence, a new thought came to Egon. If he got up, the Blackshirt would see the incriminating hole. No matter what happened, he had to sit here longer than the Blackshirt.

Between the paralyzing fear and controlling his expression, his hands, Egon totally missed the fact that they were slowing down to enter the station.

"Diepholz!" The conductor called.

Egon was encouraged.

Maybe he'll get off here. Surely an officer of the state secret police needs to check in with his colleagues at the train station.

No such luck.

Other bodies scurried for exits. *Other* faces sought seats alone next to windows. But the Blackshirt stayed exactly where he was, apparently quite relaxed.

Egon, however, was not the least bit comfortable.

As the train pulled away, it took him several moments to realize that something really had changed—there was a new pressure against his left hip—and another quick moment before he realized exactly what that pressure was.

The pistol.

The Blackshirt had repositioned himself and was now taking up a good portion of Egon's seat. Egon considered his options. Does the mouse criticize the hawk's manners?

He rearranged himself so that his entire body touched the wall. He had no interest in contact with even the butt end of that pistol.

With every kilometer, the tension made Egon more exhausted. He was stiff from not moving. He could no longer control the muscles in his forehead, cheeks, and eyebrows. And now he really did need to use the toilet.

Still, he didn't move. He didn't do one blessed thing. If the man next to him could stay in one place all the way to Osnabrück, Egon could too.

Finally the train came to a stop and, with as little fanfare as when he sat down, the Blackshirt left. Egon waited a moment, then lost himself in the crowd as he made his way to his next train.

The crowds, the loudspeaker, the crush of the people scurrying for the various platforms—after the tension of the railroad car, all of it was a relief. Egon stretched his arms and legs as he walked, the cool air chilling his damp body. That, too, felt good after the warmth and closeness inside the car.

Ordinarily, changing trains at an unfamiliar station would be cause for worry. With all his other concerns, Egon hardly gave it a thought.

It was only a short ride to Rheine. Still, Egon was very careful to search out the oldest, noisiest, fullest train car he could find. He chose a seat between two overweight men who had not bathed in some weeks.

It was a nice ride.

15

E xcuse me, what's the best way to Sommer
Street?''

"Bus to town." The clerk didn't even look
up. "Get off at the third stop."

"Thanks."

Almost there. As he climbed onto the bus, Egon realized
he hadn't eaten anything since early in the morning. Suddenly he was very interested in discovering what Berta had
packed him to eat. But he needed to pay attention. No
getting lost now. Egon studied the street signs, the holiday
decorations, the piles of dirty snow that lay in doorways and
next to curbs.

As if he knew what he was doing, Egon left the bus at
the third stop. He saw Sommer Street right away, one block
off the main drag. With a sudden lightness in his step, Egon
headed toward the address. Maybe he wouldn't have to wait
until tomorrow. Maybe they would leave tonight. Surely
night would be the best time to be inconspicuous. Egon
slowed a little, changing from a quick city stride to his
version of a coal miner's walk.

The movements were slower and wider. He was tired,
after all, from a long day in the mines, and he had to carry

his tools. Along with the modified trudge, he slackened his face; no longer looking from side to side with interest, he stared straight ahead, his eyes dull.

With a start, Egon realized he was not copying some imagined coal miner.

He was imitating his father.

Back to his brisk gait, Egon began searching in earnest for the address. These houses had more space around them than in the city. Their addresses were less obvious, however, and some of the post boxes had only names.

Egon walked back and forth three times before he convinced himself. This was no time to make a mistake.

The house was unremarkable, as if designed and maintained precisely to make it blend in with the others on the block. No mezuzah.

He knocked firmly.

"Yes?" Her middle-aged face was as bland as the house.

"I'm here to see Mr. Ritter."

She ushered him in and closed the door.

"Are you Mrs. Ritter?"

Her smile wasn't so bad. "No."

"My name is Eg—"

She put her hand up to stop him. "The fewer names, the better."

"Is Mr. Ritter here?"

"No." She looked him over. "I don't suppose you've eaten."

He weighed politeness against Berta's food, against the uncertainty of what was to come. "Not lately."

"Let's see if we can find something, and then I'll show you to the waiting room." She marched off. "Follow me."

The kitchen was more like his mother's than Berta's.

The woman with no name put some beans, a boiled potato, and a thick slice of dark bread onto a plate. Then she filled a pitcher of water and handed it to him.

Egon smiled. *She must think I'm awfully thirsty.*

"Follow me." And she led him up the stairs.

Despite her sternness, Egon found it hard to control his enthusiasm. As they walked, he recreated their meeting as it might have gone.

"Egon, we're so glad to see you. How was the train ride?"

"A little long. Especially while the Blackshirt was sitting next to me."

"Next to you?" She shivered and touched him sympathetically on the arm. "Don't worry, you'll be out of Germany before you know it."

They turned and headed up even narrower stairs.

"You're a baker, aren't you?"

"Apprentice baker."

"Sorry about the spare rations, but as you know, these days everything's difficult."

"I'd be happy to help in the kitchen."

"No need for that. You'll be out of here before you know it." She smiled as she looked him over. "Just last week we had a boy come through, looked a lot like you. Did just fine."

Mrs. No Name opened a door at the end of the hall.

Strange place for a waiting room. When Egon looked inside, he was even more confused.

"Keep the window shade down. Walking is okay as long as you take your shoes off and are quiet about it. There's a pot underneath the bed."

Egon blushed, glad he had taken care of that at the station.

"When do you expect Mr. Ritter?"

"Saturday."

Saturday! "But that's three days from now. . . . I thought . . ."

She turned to go. "It's better if you don't think."

16

Three days in this rat hole. Even the Levis had had a toilet. And heat.

His breath clouded the room just as it had outside. Egon didn't even consider removing his coat.

The food was as dull and old as it looked, but it clearly wasn't going to get any warmer or any fresher. The bread was dry. At least two days old. He dipped it into the water before he chewed it.

He removed his shoes and paced the small room. She hadn't said anything about the hallway, so he ventured out there as well. But that made him nervous. He returned to the room.

Three days. Egon multiplied in his head. Seventy-two hours. That sounded a little better.

As he thought about it, the truly bad part wasn't the waiting. Or the food. Or the cold. Or the confinement. Or the pot under the bed.

The worst part was the utter lack of control. Ever since he was fifteen years old, Egon had functioned as an adult—handling money, making appointments, dealing with customers. He made deliveries and he made decisions. He sent money to his mother. And when there was trouble, he went to court all alone to speak for himself.

And here he sat. Alone—which was all right—with every shred of control stripped away—which was all wrong.

Why hadn't he asked more questions about how this was going to work? Did Mrs. No Name plan to check on him occasionally? What if Mr. Ritter didn't show up on Saturday? What then? And what was going to happen after he was in Holland? Would there be another Mrs. No Name on the other side? How would he let Sam and Berta know that he'd made it safely?

Around and around the questions went until Egon's head spun like a crazy clock. Maybe Mrs. No Name was right. It would be better if he didn't think.

But what else was he to do? No work. No play. No books. No friends. No relatives. No one. No heat. For seventy-two hours, thinking was all he had.

So Egon sat back on the lumpy bed, closed his eyes, and settled on the most pleasant topic he could find.

Katarina.

Egon had known other pretty girls, of course. Right after he started with the Levis he'd taken a couple girls to films. And kissed them afterward, which was nice. Very nice.

Still, they were nothing to compare to Katarina. Her thick hair, lush brows, and lashes were very dark, just this side of black, a marvelous contrast to her fair skin. A butterfly would skid, so smooth and clear was that precious skin.

And Katarina liked him, that was the obvious part. The best part.

Because they had so little time together, Egon felt that her every look, her every gesture, was choreographed with him in mind. When she brushed a tendril of hair out of her eyes, that was for him. When she licked a crumb from her upper lip, that was for him. When her blouse was arranged so that a little extra shoulder was visible, that was definitely for him.

"Don't rush so much," she said one day. "Life is meant to be savored."

For him.

Even casual conversation, about her life at the coffee shop or his at the bakery, kept Egon whirling in a fascinated orbit around her.

"Life is so hard that sometimes it seems like everyone is angry at everyone else. Harsh words and violent thoughts are everywhere. My uncle yells at my aunt, who yells at the customers, who yell at me. It can be very discouraging.

"The other day I decided to try an experiment. Science classes have always appealed to me at school. Hydrogen and oxygen combine to make water, not just if they're in a good mood, or if it's a sunny day—but given the right conditions, oxygen and hydrogen will make water every single time.

"Other subjects aren't like that. In literature, the author may have intended this, or may have intended the other. Even in mathematics, for years and years they tell you that it's impossible to subtract ten from five. Then you get to be thirteen years old, they pull negative numbers out of some magic box where they've been hiding, and all of a sudden any fool can subtract ten from five.

"Anyway, I was getting to my experiment." Katarina had been ironing napkins that morning. "I decided that if water is always made up of hydrogen and oxygen, maybe there is a similar rule I could find out about people.

"Mr. and Mrs. Mueller certainly seem predictable

enough—just like the oxygen and hydrogen. But I decided to try and change the *conditions*.

"Oxygen and hydrogen need heat to become water. Mr. and Mrs. Mueller always seem to generate their own heat, but what if it were possible to drain that heat away before it reached combustion temperature?

"The other day, before they could shout any commands, I made it a point to say 'Good morning!' in my most cheerful voice. When they argued about which one of them would go to the bank, I offered to go instead. When they started raising their voices, I did the opposite, lowering mine so they would have to be quiet in order to hear me.

"That was the most harmonious day we've ever had. The customers sensed it and didn't make so many unreasonable demands. There were actually stray smiles around here, and Mrs. Mueller even brought up the subject of giving me a few days off next summer so I can visit my sister."

Egon had stood there, basking in her glow. Not only was her body beautiful, but her spirit was as well.

"I know how frustrated you get with the Levis," she'd said. "Maybe you could try something similar."

Egon had laughed. "Herman Levi isn't hydrogen or oxygen. He's sulfuric acid!"

Eyes closed there in the little room, Egon could remember every detail. The way her lashes reached out, as if to him. How she moved so gracefully it looked as if there were no steps involved. The way she smelled, like spring flowers after a rain.

The way her eyes and her very being seemed to embrace him.

Although her tone was beautiful and loving, her every movement was considered and appropriate. But with a touch of imagination . . .

* * *

KATARINA'S BLOUSE SLIPPED a little farther. He could feel her butterfly skin, and her hands on him. The Muellers' kitchen was gone, and it was summer. Just the two of them in a field of wildflowers.

Katarina picked a miniature violet and used it to caress his face. Starting at his forehead, she moved in small circles down his cheek, past his ear to his neck. Her face was right behind, tracing the path of the flower with soft breaths, so faint he almost couldn't be sure, except that he was. And then the flower was gone and it was only her breath, and then her lips, grazing his neck.

Gracefully his shirt was shoved aside as her tongue joined the slow southward dance.

He massaged her back, experiencing fully every perfect movement. There was no space between the two of them. The feeling was everything he'd always imagined it would be, but better. Now her hands joined in, disregarding clothing as easily as the bounds of propriety. Never had skin felt so smooth, so eager, so right.

Abruptly she stopped the flirting and met him, mouth to mouth, in a hard kiss. Hearts pounding, eyes open, it was impossible to say who was making love to whom.

EGON'S EYES FLEW OPEN. He adjusted his pants.

If everything went as planned, he wouldn't see Katarina Mueller again, probably for years. Maybe never. Mrs. No Name was right. Thinking only made it worse.

17

Egon woke with a start. Why was he wearing his clothes? His coat? Herman Levi would have his skin for sleeping until it was light.

Reality came back in a second. There was nothing Herman Levi could dish out, however, that could compare to the unpleasantnesses conjured up by Egon's imagination.

At least it was morning. At least he had made it through the night. Surely Mrs. No Name would return this morning. Egon had spent the long hours before he fell asleep making up a list of questions for her. Surely she—or someone— would be here soon. They couldn't expect him to last three days on that stuff from last night. Not that he wasn't grateful. But then, how grateful did he need to be? Surely Mr. Ritter, Mrs. No Name, and all the other Mr. and Mrs. No Names were going to be well recompensed.

Egon reached down to the hem of his coat. His money was still in place.

Where was that woman anyway? How could such a large house stay so quiet? Were there other miners stashed in other waiting rooms? Did any of them ever die of frostbite?

What time Saturday?

With every minute his list of questions grew. What if there was no Mr. Ritter? What if it was all an elaborate ruse, a plot to steal money from desperate people? What would happen if he got caught? This was the question on which Egon never allowed himself to dwell.

For perhaps the fiftieth time he scanned the small room. *Damn.*

How could he have slept through the most important moments of the morning? That wasn't good. He would have to train himself to sleep more lightly.

There on the shelf next to the window was the evidence of Mrs. No Name's visit. Bread. Coffee with milk. A fresh pitcher of water. A bowl of thin stew. A piece of sausage.

Egon frowned at the large quantity. A meal like this now meant he couldn't expect another visit for some time, certainly not before supper, maybe even tomorrow morning.

He dipped a finger into the coffee. Still hot. He'd overslept by just minutes.

What the meal possessed in quantity it lacked in quality. But since Egon had absolutely no idea when—if?—there would be more, he ate every bite.

Egon stared again at the small room and the long stretch ahead of him. Was this confinement merely a prelude to a more real imprisonment? Egon shook his head. That kind of thinking would make it a very long two days.

Carefully he poured a splash of water into the washbowl. The soap was brown and hard and didn't lather. But even to himself Egon didn't complain. No matter what happened, he was in charge of the here and now. He couldn't relive the scooter accident. He couldn't understand or change the rules that had affected every detail of his life for as long as he could remember. But even here, even now, he was the master of his own thoughts. It might be brown and hard but, Egon consciously decided, he was fortunate to have soap of any kind.

In one quick movement Egon shucked his coat and threw it onto the bed.

Instantly all vestiges of sleep were frozen out of him. Sleeves up, his arms were dotted with goose bumps.

Egon washed hands and face, and made a brisk pass at his underarms. He'd already decided to save his clean shirt, socks, and underwear for Saturday. *Brrr*. At least he could roll his sleeves down for the next part.

The razor next to Berta's package in his satchel reminded Egon that there were still people out there who cared about him. Reassuring as that thought was, he had business to attend to.

Egon did his best to make a lather with the soap and frigid water. If he cut himself, his face would be numb. At least he wouldn't bleed to death. Once he started in, however, Egon wasn't so sure. Sam's razor was a little different, and a lot sharper. Egon had to tip the handle at an unusual angle. And the shivering didn't help. Eventually he figured out that it worked best if he took a deep breath before each stroke.

Still, it was an arduous process. He was glad he didn't yet have to shave every day.

Coat finally on again, Egon breathed a little easier. He peered outside near the edge of the window shade. Sunshine. That was unusual. There were very few people out, and Egon realized it was much later than he had thought.

It could be any house, on any street, in any town. That, obviously, was the point.

A hundred times around the room. That would be a good start. And as he walked in his stocking feet, Egon remembered the list of prepositions he'd memorized as a twelve-year-old.

Aboard . . . about . . . above . . . across . . . after . . .

against . . . before . . . behind . . . beneath . . . beside
. . between . . . beyond . . . by . . . down . . . during
. . . except . . . for . . . from. . . .

One preposition for every two laps of the room. Fifty
prepositions. A hundred laps. No time at all.

Egon had been a good student. Particularly in the early
years, the teachers had appreciated his attentiveness, his
inquisitiveness, and his ingenuity. Egon remembered with
pride that even after other factors had made school less than
pleasant, he'd gotten the highest scores in chemistry and
Latin.

sum
es
est
sumus
estis
sunt

Egon liked Latin. The words were both grand and precise. And unlike other subjects, where political factors could
so easily become a part of the lesson, Latin was different.
The subjunctive was always the subjunctive and the indicative was always the indicative. Hitler or no. And besides,
Egon was good at languages.

He liked English too. The rules were more difficult to
remember. No, it wasn't the rules, but the *exceptions* to the
rules that were a pain. And unlike Latin or Hebrew, English
was a living language, and that made him feel connected to
the world outside Germany.

I am.
You are.
He is.
They are. . . .

His brother Carl and his sister Sidonie spoke English

every day now. Perhaps they said the lines he'd learned from Mrs. Fischer.

The little boy pulls the red wagon through the mysterious woods.

Please, I would like two tickets to the matinee.

He tried to remember exactly what the sentences meant. *Matinee* gave him trouble. *Mat* was easy. That meant a small square, as for wiping the feet. Perhaps a matinee was a fancy kind of mat.

Please, I would like two tickets to the doormat. That made no sense at all. So much for English.

Egon peeked outside again. More people this time. It was the middle of the day, dinnertime. Egon wasn't hungry, but he remembered the snack Berta had packed for him— was it only yesterday?—and realized that, hungry or not, he'd better eat it, or it would spoil.

With forty-eight hours still to go, Egon was in no hurry about anything.

He stared at the folded paper square for a long time, determined to extend any small pleasure it might contain. He decided to guess what was inside. The brown paper was darker where grease from inside had soaked through. He sniffed. Cheese. Probably a little stiff, but still edible.

No sweets, surely. They weren't sturdy enough food and, besides, despite her formerly high-quality oven, Berta was no baker. Egon felt the paper. To go with the cheese, there was probably a roll or a chunk of bread, and a piece of wurst or sausage.

Although he really wasn't hungry, Egon's mouth was wet with anticipation. Slowly he folded back the corners.

Egon smiled. He was right. Suddenly hungry, he was just about to reach inside when he noticed something else. A piece of paper.

Dear Egon,

Our hearts are with you. Our love and our prayers are with you. Don't think about what you've left behind. Keep your head up, your mind clear, and think about a future where everyone can live together in harmony. We will see you there soon.

Love, Berta

Egon read and reread the note, searching for some clue as to why it should fill him with such despair.

18

Y ou must know more than you're telling me."
Egon stood so that his body blocked the door.
Mrs. No Name stood inside his room, trapped
and unhappy.

"I've told you, I haven't the faintest idea." The woman
glanced about quickly, looking for an opening.

Did she expect him just to sit up here like a child and
not even ask a question? Two days' worth of anger and
frustration gave determination to his wide stance.

Mrs. No Name was equally adamant. For ten minutes
they had stood there. "I told you I don't know *anything*."
Her voice softened slightly. "And I don't *want* to know
anything."

With that Egon's resistance crumbled. He didn't want
to battle Mrs. No Name. He wanted Otto Sprage. He wanted
the judge. He wanted the kids who'd thrown rocks at him
and the teachers who had encouraged it. He wanted the
people who passed the laws, the ones who painted swastikas
in the night. The anonymous voices who broadcast hate at
the train stations.

He wanted Julie. He wanted his father and his brothers
and sisters, and everything to be as it had been when he was
small. Not enough money or food certainly, but plenty of

love, and older siblings and parents ready and willing to right any wrong.

Egon was alone again. Food on the table. Stench in the air.

He'd meant to ask her to change the pot, but he couldn't blame her for slipping away at the first opportunity.

Except for the cold, the smell would have been impossible to bear. The cold and the smell and his coat were a part of him, like his own smell. A miner should smell, though, shouldn't he?

Tomorrow was Saturday. Tomorrow Mr. Ritter would come. Tomorrow he would leave Germany. That was the thought that sustained him as he remembered his last years at school.

EGON WAS TWELVE when he started riding the train to high school every day in Lemgo. He felt so grown-up then, so proud in his new cap that signified his class ranking. He was agile, and his small size helped him as a gymnast. He was recognized both for that and for his academic ability.

Lotte Nolting, August Timmer, Alex Ueckermann, Ernest Laufhager, and all the others from Barntrup sat together on the train for the one-hour ride to Lemgo. Egon knew it wasn't just friendliness that inspired the camaraderie—it was his perfectly completed homework assignments, which were hastily passed around and copied each morning. Allowing them to cheat was a small concession that assured him firm membership in the group. For a while.

He never knew exactly when, or why, everything became so different. One day there was simply a picture of the führer on the wall behind every teacher's desk. Nothing was said. Nothing else changed. Probably the other kids didn't even notice. They still went every day from class to class, complaining about this teacher, passing rumors about the other one. They still snatched one another's lunches and they still copied Egon's homework.

For a long time Egon had known that he was different from all the other students. Egon acknowledged that difference and attributed it to his more sincere interest in schoolwork. Egon actually liked his lessons, particularly Dr. Ulrich Walters's class in English literature. The man was an educated gentleman, somewhat stern but impeccably fair. Egon loved to listen to him talk. His graceful, fluid sentences reached out in an unfamiliar, almost seductive, way. He could get to the essence of a subject, and in such a way that his students never felt forced to learn. But learn Egon did. Especially in the lessons on Gilbert Chesterton. From the moment he heard it, one of Chesterton's sentences stood out in bald relief for him. "When men run in packs, they lose their sense of decency."

Why else was Egon the butt of an increasing number of jokes? Why else the occasional rock flung his way? Egon didn't tell anyone, and he certainly didn't complain, knowing instinctively that calling attention to the situation would only make it worse. Julie had always cautioned him against fighting, but Egon knew that if it came to that, he would be able to defend himself, and then some.

Not like Papa. . . . Papa had been so proud of his membership in the veterans' organization. He had thought that that special green veteran's cap made the other men see him—a cattle and hog trader—as their equal. Why Papa cared about drinking beer and singing songs with those old goats was a separate issue, but he obviously did. Papa had chosen to ignore the asides, the none-too-subtle hints, until finally the day came when he was told outright that he was no longer welcome at the veterans' meeting. How he whined and fussed—not outside the house, of course—but Egon remembered having very little patience with him, wanting to be as far away and as different as possible from that father of his.

On cold reflection, however, he and Papa were not so different. Papa had thought that his veterans' association cap was a lifelong sign of approval. Egon had thought that being generous with his homework would win him acceptance.

Even when the teasing grew worse, when politics entered the classroom, when anti-Semitism became a part of the official curriculum, Egon ignored it. He rode alone on the train then, and he ignored that too. He did not dwell on the brown shirts and shoulder straps worn by the enthusiastic young student Nazis. And when his older brother Carl suggested that Egon quit school to learn a trade, he didn't listen. Carl's persistence, and their other brothers' support for the idea, was a betrayal that made him both angry and determined. He was not quitting school. He was going to college.

But that was before *Ivanhoe*.

UNLIKE DR. WALTERS the previous year, Ludwig Betz had few academic qualifications. A relatively new teacher at the Lemgo high school, Mr. Betz was often ridiculed, for both his club foot and his harsh southern accent. His politics were correct, however, and Mr. Betz maintained impeccable discipline.

The major project of the spring semester was the reading and discussion of Sir Walter Scott's *Ivanhoe*.

Even Mr. Betz could not ruin the book for Egon. Such a story! Castles and fair maidens, chivalrous knights willing to fight and die on behalf of the ladies. There was treachery, trickery, and enough heroism for three ordinary books. So much of what they had to read was so boring, or preachy, that even though *Ivanhoe* was difficult, it was a pleasure: an actual story.

Despite the snide remarks, despite the fact that Mr. Betz picked on him, Egon found himself looking forward to the class, anxious to hear about the cool, green English countryside. The feudal system was intriguing. And once he heard that Sir Walter Scott had had a limp, Egon realized that perhaps there was good reason why their teacher felt a kinship with the author.

Mr. Betz used the book as an excuse for an extended lecture on the Crusades, "an admirable effort to drive infidels from the birthplace of our Lord." The Crusades had not been successful, according to Mr. Betz, and had been motivated in large part by the glory that they brought to their leaders. It was an intriguing idea that Egon carried a step further—for hundreds and hundreds of years, political leaders had been using religion as an excuse to do whatever they pleased.

"And for the conclusion of our study of *Ivanhoe*, I have planned a special treat."

Everyone in the class leaned forward. For Mr. Betz to use two words they'd never heard from him—*special* and *treat*—was quite a surprise.

"I have planned a debate on the characters in *Ivanhoe*."

"Let Lotte be Lady Rowena," someone called out.

A response was instant. "But Lady Rowena is supposed to be virtuous!"

Mr. Betz glared around the room, looking for the fool unwise enough to say such a thing in his class.

No luck. For once the students were utterly still. Several times each day Mr. Betz pounded his cane on the floor, seeking to be heard. This time, however, the class had the wisdom to fall silent of its own accord.

"Uh-hm." Mr. Betz was clearly impatient to move on. "A debate on two of the characters: Isaac and Rebecca." He paused. "Which one is a more accurate representation of the Jew? Egon Katz will take the part of Rebecca. August Timmer will speak about Isaac. The winner will be determined by student vote." Mr. Betz spoke quickly. "The debate will be a week from today. Dismissed."

The class heaved a collective sigh. All they had to do was listen. Egon was pleased. Finally, a fight his mother wouldn't object to. And August Timmer was an idiot. A well-liked idiot, but an idiot nonetheless.

For that week Egon turned into a veritable scholar. He had kept assuming . . . hoping . . . that people would notice he did not fit the caricature of the Jew portrayed in the newspapers. Now he had been given a platform, not merely to hope, but to explain, and with virtuous Rebecca as the representative of Judaism. What an opportunity!

Papa hadn't seen it that way. "A little help from you around here, that's all I ask."

"But Papa, this is important."

"Does *Rebecca*"—he spat it out—"put food on the table? Does she? At your age I was working. Your brothers are all gone off to their fancy jobs. I work every daylight hour. And what about you, Egon? All day long you sit there, with an audience of papers and books. It looks like laziness to me."

"But Papa—"

"Max, leave him alone," Julie interrupted.

Egon was astonished. It was rare, indeed, for his mother to stand up to his father.

"Egon does very well in school. And he works hard at it. I *won't* have you calling him lazy."

"He's always the baby for you. Nobody notices how hard I work around here. Some stupid lesson is important, but my hard work is not!" He slammed the door.

Egon had worked even harder, rereading the book, searching out library references at lunch, organizing and reorganizing his notes. Egon not only had to convince his class and Mr. Betz, he apparently had to convince his own father.

The day of the debate was cold and dreary, but not to Egon. For once he was glad to be alone on the train. To himself he mouthed the words and marked out the gestures that would help him make his points. He had always been comfortable with public speaking. And he had never looked forward so much to a class, particularly a class with Mr. Betz. For once he was going to be able to use logic and clear thinking against muddy arguments that usually lurked in shadows.

Egon couldn't help smiling. It was as if his entire school career had been a preparation for today.

August Timmer, too, was smiling.

Egon shook his head slightly. August was only a mediocre student, a would-be soldier who made no secret of his impatience with academics. Mr. Betz should have chosen a more worthy adversary.

At his desk, Egon realized that all the students were in a jovial mood. Of course. They hadn't had to prepare for today's class, and besides, it was always fun to watch one of their own make a fool of himself in front of the class.

Mr. Betz rapped his cane on the floor for quiet. "I'm sure you all remember the debate we have planned for today. The question is, Which is the more accurate representation of the Jewish race, Isaac of York, or his daughter, Rebecca the Jewess?

"Speaking for Rebecca we have Egon Katz. On the side of Isaac we have August Timmer." Mr. Betz tapped his cane. "Katz will go first."

The class was polite. Although he did not plan to refer to them, Egon placed his carefully detailed notes on the podium.

He looked confidently out at the classroom. "While some might say it is unfair, or even dangerous, to judge an entire group of people based on one member, Rebecca is indeed a brilliant example of the best of Judaism." Egon pointedly avoided the heavy slang dialect he spoke with his friends. This was an argument that required High German.

"Both the characters in the story and we, the readers of it, are impressed with her beauty. Far more important, however, is Rebecca's dignity and nobility, her concern for others, and her generosity in sharing her healing works." Egon began speaking louder to make himself heard over the rustle of his classmates. "She is also firm in her righteousness. Rather than submit to the advances of Brian de Bois-Guilbert she even threatens to jump from the tower—"

"She should have jumped!"

Egon didn't see the speaker. Mr. Betz's cane was still. He made no attempt to quiet the ensuing commotion.

There was more to say about Rebecca, but Egon didn't have that much time. He cleared his throat pointedly and attempted to continue. "In a few minutes August Timmer will speak about Isaac of York. Before he does, I would like to say a few words about him.

"For hundreds of years Christians were barred by church leaders from banking and were forbidden to be merchants. So it was only natural for Jews to fill that gap. A few, like

Isaac, became overly greedy. Yes, Isaac loves money to a fault. And in his greed and wickedness, I argue that Isaac is the unfortunate and isolated exception. But more than money, Isaac loves his daughter.''

They were actually booing and hissing. Egon struggled with disbelief as he tried to finish. ''It is Rebecca who is the shining example. She maintains her faith despite adversity. She restores Gurth's money when it is the right thing to do. Her strength of character and wisdom far outshadow any failing of her father's when she says''—Egon glanced at his paper to get the quote right—'' 'We are like the herb which flourisheth most when it is trampled upon.' ''

Egon's cheeks flamed as he left the front of the room. They were laughing, heckling him. When he returned to his desk, Egon noticed that his ink bottle had been turned over on his books.

He wanted to go a couple of rounds with the kid in the next row. He wanted to hurt him—to hurt them all—and never mind the dignity and righteousness of Rebecca.

Instead, he swallowed hard and took another seat.

''Thank you,'' said the teacher, ''that was quite . . . illuminating. Timmer?''

August Timmer grabbed the podium as if he owned it.

''So Rebecca enjoys being trampled upon?'' He paused for effect. ''I will be happy to oblige.'' There was laughter as August ground his boot heel into the floor.

Egon's anger evaporated into despair. There was nothing he could do to right matters. He had grown up with these classmates. Now, apparently, he was simply an object of scorn. How had it happened? What had he done wrong?

From the unfamiliar seat Egon watched the black ink. Drip. Drip.

His books were ruined. The debate was lost. Friends. He had none.

August Timmer's words were an assault.

"As for Isaac's feelings for his daughter, well, even vermin love their children. But parent or child, they are vermin nonetheless." The crowd was warming up. "Isaac of York is the Jew we have learned to hate. He is greedy, unattractive, whining, and devious. And he manipulates every situation to his own advantage."

The class was now nodding and silent.

"Isaac's ancestors killed our Lord Jesus Christ, and Isaac is no better than they were. . . ."

Does this, thought Egon, have anything to do with *Ivanhoe*? Or the debate? But what came next was an even greater departure from the subject. It was Nazi hate propaganda, pure and simple. August preached it. The teacher allowed it. And the students wallowed in it.

"Parasites like the Jew Isaac are unfit to share the glorious Germanic heritage." August put his hands up for quiet. "I do, however, agree with the Jew Katz on one thing. It is important to close with a quote. This is from the editorial page of the newspaper last week: 'The only things the Jews understand are the pistol and the whip. We will spare them neither.'"

TWO WEEKS LATER Egon had become a baker's apprentice.

19

By now, cold water and tepid breakfast had become a routine. No news from Mrs. No Name. The same drab walls, the same frigid air. But today was different. Today was Saturday.

Egon shaved carefully. Moving quickly, he washed as well as he could and changed into his clean clothes. He dipped his hands into the water, then ran them through his light-brown hair.

Glancing first at the aged mirror, Egon tucked his shirt in more firmly, hoping to rid it of some of its wrinkles. He had barely finished when there was a light knock at the door. Mrs. No Name must have forgotten something.

"Good morning."

Egon stood there, dumb as a fence post. His dirty clothes—and his coat—were strewn on the bed.

Mr. Ritter. Three days to prepare for this moment, and Egon wasn't ready. Awkwardly he extended his right hand. "Good morning, sir."

Mr. Ritter—a large, heavy-muscled man—just stood there, staring.

Dozens of questions jostled for Egon's attention, but he hesitated. Would it be better to speak the proper High German his mother was so proud of? Or the dialect of the streets? High German was probably better. He could always switch later. Still Egon hesitated. His life depended on the man in front of him. "It's good to meet you, Mr. Ritter."

The man nodded. "Let's have a look at you." Motioning Egon to the far corner, Mr. Ritter crossed the room in three steps and raised the window shade.

Egon cringed, at both the bright light and the forbidden action. But the man moved with authority and utter confidence, the first reassuring traits Egon had seen in days. The man was experienced. Surely he knew what he was doing.

"When do we leave?" Egon was impatient.

Mr. Ritter stood back, peering at him from all angles. "The guards are getting tougher."

Egon glanced quickly, longingly, at his coat.

He was being examined—as he had once examined cows with his father.

But that was fine. Egon had nothing to be ashamed of. He stood proud at five feet six inches. His eyes were blue, his face, wide and unblemished, with a nose too small to be thought Jewish. His face was what had allowed Egon to live undisturbed for so long.

As he stood, still and proud, Egon's only concern was the intense cold. He tensed and flexed his muscles in an attempt to stave off uncontrollable shivering.

Mr. Ritter appeared not to notice the cold. But then, he was wearing a coat.

"Walk for me."

Suddenly self-conscious in his stocking feet, Egon walked out to the hall and back

Mr. Ritter nodded.

Was his walk acceptable? What was the man looking for?

"Now, your hands." Mr. Ritter took Egon's hands in

his own, turned them this way and that, staring hard at the nails and the palms.

Egon's hands were strong and broad, accustomed to hard work. But as Egon looked at them with Mr. Ritter's eyes, he noted the fair, unblemished skin, and the complete lack of calluses, with consternation.

Finally Mr. Ritter sat down on the bed.

His expression was one Egon had seen often enough on his father. Coarse as he had appeared on the surface, Max Katz always hated to dispense unpleasant news. But there had been a great deal of it over the years: the foal the mare was carrying was stillborn . . . the sheep had anthrax.

Worst of all is the bad news you are holding your breath for: the boy is going to prison.

Egon forced himself to listen.

"I'm very sorry." Mr. Ritter spoke slowly. "It's not me. In the last week the border guards have become very suspicious. You're strong, yes, but you are finely featured. You're obviously young." He paused. "How old are you?"

Egon swallowed hard. "Twenty-one."

Mr. Ritter looked down. "No one would ever believe that those hands swing a pickax every day."

"I'll wear work gloves."

"It's not just that. Your face is a little . . . delicate. You don't look like a miner."

"What's a miner look like?" Egon switched to the more guttural form of speech. "I'll rub dirt into my face. Get some different clothes. I know how to curse!"

Mr. Ritter shook his head. "You'd be risking more than your own life. I have to think about all the others."

The cold had penetrated into every particle of his body. But that didn't matter. Nothing mattered.

"I'm sorry."

He shook Egon's uncallused hand.

"You're a clever young man. You'll figure out something. I'm truly sorry." And he was gone.

20

Sorry. *Sorry?*

Coat once again on his *delicate* shoulders—
no, it was his face that was delicate—Egon angrily paced the room.

What was he going to do?

Egon shoved away the emotions that threatened to overwhelm him. As he began methodically stuffing dirty clothes back into his satchel, he realized that he had not a glimmer of an idea what he would do, where he would go.

As Mr. Ritter had said, it wasn't just his own life. He would be putting anyone he contacted at risk. Surely the Blackshirts would have turned his room at the Levis' upside down. His name and description—smooth hands, delicate face—were surely on all the lists now. Sam and Berta had been generous, but he couldn't go back there. More than anything else, he wanted to see his mother. But that, too, was out of the question.

Who would know what to do?

As soon as he asked himself the question, Egon knew the answer.

Bruno.

Bruno would know what to do. Bruno was four years older than Egon, a teacher in a Jewish day school. Perhaps more important, Bruno had been talking for months about leaving Germany. Before, Egon had always dismissed Bruno's concerns. But if anyone would know what to do, it would be Bruno.

Bruno lived in Hamburg, a full day away on the train.

Egon glanced quickly around the room, then headed down the stairs. Mrs. No Name was nowhere to be seen. Egon swore to himself that never again would he put himself at the mercy of a Mrs. No Name, or his life in the hands of someone he had never met. Modest as his talents were, they were his alone. And who could be more motivated than Egon himself to save his skin?

As he headed down the front steps, Egon realized that this time, for better or for worse, he was really on his own.

THE FIRST STAGE OF HIS TRIP, retracing the way to Bremen, was difficult. With every revolution of the train's wheels he came closer to that arrest warrant. Or was it a death warrant?

The ride was long, but eventful only in the despair with which Egon experienced it. There were Blackshirts, but they patrolled the more comfortable cars. There were crying children, but Egon was not tempted to sing to them.

The more he thought about it, the grimmer the situation appeared. Bruno was not going to have any magic answers. If he did, he would already have left himself.

Still, Bruno and Hamburg was the only reasonable goal Egon could think of, and so he headed toward it.

It was dark when he reached the Hamburg train station. Bruno's apartment was only a short walk. Christmas decorations brightened store windows, and Egon realized for the first time that the next night was the first night of Hanukkah.

He didn't feel like lighting any candles.

21

It was winter break, so Bruno and Egon studied maps day and night. Bruno asked his friends for advice. The brothers considered dozens of options.

"We could probably get you to South America or South Africa," said Bruno one night.

"But I don't have documents," Egon reminded him.

"There are ways around that."

"How?"

"Forgery or bribery."

"Oh."

"But just because it's possible doesn't mean it's wise." Bruno tapped a pencil on the table.

On the one hand, Egon respected his older brother's knowledge. On the other, every day, every minute, in Germany increased the chance that he would be apprehended. Thoughts of prison tortured every calm moment. Just when he began to spiral off in fear, Egon would rein himself back in. Surely he was exaggerating the risk. Even if they were looking for him, it had to be in a passive sort of way. But for Egon there was nothing passive about the present. Every ounce of creativity and initiative he had ever possessed focused on one goal. Egon had to believe that his single-minded efforts would be more effective than the creeping fingers of government.

"If you were a little younger, we might be able to get you to England."

"England?"

"A consortium of churches plan to evacuate Jewish children to England."

Egon digested the information. How young would he have to be? Sixteen? Fourteen? If he was obviously too delicate to be a coal miner, maybe it would be possible. There was still the problem of papers. Did churches take bribes?

Egon realized that Bruno was staring at him, clearly deciding whether to say something.

"Gertrud is sending Susan."

Egon was confused. Their sister was *sending* their niece? That made her sound like a parcel. "Sending Susan where?"

"To England."

"But Susan is only eight." Every time Egon turned around, the situation seemed worse. "She's going alone?"

Bruno nodded.

"They'll try to convert her," said Egon. Why did that bother him so much?

"The *only* important thing is that Susan will be safe."

Egon's head hurt. Each time he thought he had considered everything, there was a new rock with ever more disgusting bugs underneath. Egon wanted to understand. He wanted to get out of here, under his own steam. But he had to be careful. He'd been ignoring Bruno's increasingly ominous hints for several days.

Bruno had been in prison. He obviously knew more than he was telling.

Egon stared at the brother whom people always said he resembled. He wanted to know—he needed to know—whatever Bruno knew.

"Bruno"—Egon summoned courage from all directions—"there's something you're not telling me."

Bruno stared into space and tapped his pencil furiously on the maps. "It's about Leni."

"Leni?" What could she possibly have to do with his getting out of Germany?

"Do you really think Leni fell into a ditch?"

Leni, sweet Leni, who always mended his torn pants without letting their mother see the rips. . . . Leni, who could always make their mother smile. He couldn't believe it had been a year and a half since he'd seen her. "Something happened to her."

"Yes, *something* did happen to her. But where's her body? It's been eighteen months. If there'd been an accident, surely someone would have come across her body. And why wouldn't the police make even token inquiries into her whereabouts?"

Egon was more confused than ever. Leni's death had been terrible, but it was finished, not something he had thought to puzzle over the way Bruno had.

"Do you think Leni would have simply wandered away?"

Egon shook his head.

"Or fallen in a ditch?"

Again Egon shook his head. "Then what happened to her?"

"I'm not sure." Bruno stabbed his pencil point into the papers. "Maybe the police knew where she was all along. That's why they refused to investigate."

"What?"

"Think about it. Someone like Leni would be very easy to manipulate. If the police wanted her to do something, she'd obey without a question."

"But what could they possibly want with her?"

Bruno shrugged. "Nothing good." The point was broken now, and still he stabbed the pencil. "The rumors are vicious."

"Rumors about Leni?"

"Not specifically. But surely you've heard stories. . . ."

Egon had not.

"Forcing people to work against their will. Raping. Killing for sport."

"But why?"

"Because the person is Jewish."

Egon ground his fingertips into his temples.

"The reason I'm telling you this is because we have to stop deluding ourselves. The situation is worse than any of us knows. Every time something happens—they take away our driver's licenses, we can't go swimming at the public pool—and we think, That's it, it can't get any worse than this. But that's wrong. It is going to get worse—a lot worse. Do you think once we all have identification papers that say Sara or Israel the government will be content?"

Egon shrugged. "Probably not." On the other hand, he couldn't imagine a worse situation than the one he was facing.

"It's good that you're leaving, but I'd feel a lot more comfortable if you weren't all alone."

"Then come with me!"

Bruno was silent.

"Please. You're the one who's been wanting to leave. Let's go together. Right now."

Bruno looked down.

"It doesn't have to be tomorrow. If China's a good choice, I could hide out here until we can arrange passage."

"That would take weeks."

"Then let's go—go anywhere—tomorrow. There's nothing holding you here." Egon gestured toward the austere surroundings.

He suddenly focused, however, on Bruno's reticence. "Is there something holding you here?"

"There's Sabina."

"Sabina?"

"We haven't known each other long." He hesitated. "But I hope to introduce her to Mama before we leave."

Egon wondered briefly which "we" Bruno was referring to. "Do I get to be introduced as well?"

"Certainly. It's just that, for now, we need to think about getting you out of here."

Yes, that. It always startled Egon that he could forget his predicament even for a second.

"Guess I'll be doing this on my own, just like I've done everything else on my own." Egon glared at his brother, dredging up an old hurt. If he was angry at Bruno, it might be easier to leave. "I didn't get to go to college, if you remember. My brothers thought it wasn't a good idea."

"It wasn't a good idea." Bruno's voice was flat.

"For you and Carl and Herbert, college was a fine idea. For me? No."

"The world has changed in the last few years. What was good for us was not good for you."

"Is that the real reason, or were all of you afraid I'd show you up?" Egon let the bitterness creep into his imitation of his older brother. "Mama, Papa, don't let Egon go to college. He'll be better off as a baker."

"And you *are* better off as a baker." Bruno's voice was matter-of-fact. "I am a teacher in a Jewish school. What good is that going to do in China or South America, or anywhere else? But a baker—anywhere you go, people will want bread."

Egon was not ready to admit that his brother was right, but at the moment Bruno was his only ally.

22

"Y ou must know something else," Egon insisted.

Bruno shrugged. "His name is Heinz Rosenthal. He's twenty-one years old. And, if anything, he's more desperate to escape than you are. He's already spent two months in prison."

"Why?"

"Does it matter?"

Egon was firm. "I don't want to trust my life to a murderer."

"Still don't get it, do you, little brother? Maybe he flirted with a Gentile girl. Maybe his father is an outspoken rabbi. Maybe he had a scooter accident. Whatever the excuse, he was in prison because he's Jewish." He paused. "Just like you're supposed to be in jail because you're Jewish."

And I was in jail because I'm Jewish, Egon added to himself, but Bruno never mentioned that—refused, in fact, to talk about his own prison experience at all.

Bruno was right. Egon hadn't thought much about the magnitude of the problem. Clearly it wasn't just Egon and his family. It was every Jewish person in Germany.

But as he buttoned his coat, Egon hesitated. "Are you sure it's safe?"

"Either he has to come here, or you have to go there. It's definitely safer for you. If anyone stops you, say that you're me." Bruno smiled as he led Egon to the door. "If Mama can't tell us apart, no one else should be expected to."

"So, Heinz Rosenthal, where do you want to go?" For several minutes Heinz and Egon had stared across the room, taking each other's measure.

"Doesn't really matter." Heinz's shrug gave way to a smile. "Somewhere with pretty girls."

Egon liked Heinz right away. He was tall, fair-haired, and sturdy-looking. Egon had to suppress a smile when he noticed several calluses on his compatriot's hands.

As they chatted about their hometowns, sports, their school years, everything except *the subject*, Egon realized how long it had been since he'd had a friend. Someone to joke with, do things with. Someone he'd willingly trust with his life.

Finally it was time. Heinz's maps had clearly been studied just as thoroughly as Bruno's. South Africa. Scandinavia. South America. The possibilities were far-flung.

"But you realize," said Heinz, "that you can't take your money."

"No money? That's crazy." Even sitting here, knowing that his coat was on the chair not five feet away gave Egon reassurance.

"Ten marks each," said Heinz. "That's it. Crossing the border with more is a currency violation. If we get caught, I don't want that on top of everything else."

"That's not enough for a bribe. We won't get far on ten marks."

"Maybe"—Heinz's hesitation turned to a smile—"except we won't really be traveling on money. We'll be traveling on good looks and good luck.''

"And desperation.''

"That too.''

The longer they talked, the more natural the choice seemed to be. Sweden was not so far away. There were regular boats, so they wouldn't have to engage in any cloak-and-dagger tactics to get there. And although neither of them knew much about the place, neither had they heard anything bad.

"The only thing I know,'' said Heinz, "is that Swedish women are very beautiful.''

"Sounds good to me.'' Egon acted more jovial than he felt.

So it was settled. They would go to Sweden on Sunday. Christmas Day. It would be good luck. The authorities would be too preoccupied to be concerned with two young traveling men, if they noticed them at all.

Meantime, they would read everything they could find on Sweden. On Saturday morning they would get together for a final meeting to confirm where they would go once they arrived.

Egon stood to leave. Soon there would be no more peeking around doorways. No more panic at the sight of black. And this time, no putting himself at the mercy of someone he'd never even met, someone who might change his mind at the last minute.

Heinz was solid. Heinz was determined. And Heinz had enough self-confidence for the both of them. Determined as he had been not to depend on anyone else, Egon was very glad Bruno had found Heinz. Finally, something was going smoothly. When they got to Sweden, maybe Egon would even start his own bakery.

"Egon, there's something I need to tell you." Solid Heinz stared at the floor.

"Don't worry about it." Egon had decided that it was none of his business why Heinz had been in prison.

"No, really." Heinz looked even more grim. "If we are going to trust each other with our lives, we need to be truthful."

"Heinz, it doesn't matter."

"I lied to you before. . . . That matters." Heinz spoke quickly, before he lost courage. "I'm not really twenty-one. I'm only seventeen years old."

Egon suppressed a smile. "I was twenty-one once, for a few minutes. Didn't make a bit of difference."

23

As he walked along the busy street, Egon's satchel felt light. Inside was a map of Sweden and a city map of Stockholm. More important was the name Bruno's contacts had found them—Sigrid Erickson. Egon and Heinz would go to her house tomorrow evening when they arrived. Mrs. Erickson would help them find a permanent place to live and jobs—calluses or no calluses.

"Good morning," a pedestrian called out.

"Good morning," Egon replied.

The street was jammed with last-minute shoppers, all a little harried, but cheerful nonetheless. Good to see strangers with smiles on their faces.

Egon's situation hadn't changed, but his attitude certainly had.

Time was strange. Hard to believe it had been only a week since those three days in Rheine. Three weeks to the day since the scooter accident. Only one more day until he and Heinz would be free. Bruno would go this afternoon and buy their tickets. Tomorrow at this time, they would be on a ship.

Around the corner, and he would be at Heinz's apartment building.

This time Egon didn't flinch at the sight of black.

Strange to think he was apparently becoming accustomed to life as a fugitive. He stopped and stood inconspicuously, studying the newsstand headlines.

The Blackshirt stood, rifle over his shoulder, near the entrance to Heinz's building.

There were all types of newspapers. There were the party papers that preached hate. There were the local papers, papers put out by churches, and then there was the *Hamburg News*, with the largest circulation in the region. Each stack was protected from the wind by a square of iron the size of a man's forearm.

A quick glance across the street. Now there were two of them, chatting and smoking by the steps, obviously in no hurry to move on.

Egon was patient.

Not much business at the newsstand today. Egon was careful to avoid eye contact with the proprietor, a short man whose generous belly was made larger by the heavy change belt he wore around it.

Egon studied the headlines as he pretended to make a selection. JEWS OUT screamed the party headline.

Glancing about to make sure the proprietor wasn't watching, Egon moved the iron square to cover the words.

Egon picked up a copy of the *Hamburg News*. The main story was about "winter help." The idea was that once each week, every family should, instead of its usual fare, have a modest one-dish meal for dinner, with the savings to be passed along to the party. That money, so they said, would allow the boys in uniform to eat better.

Accompanying the story were large photographs of two smiling families, enjoying dinners of what looked like porridge.

Egon kept his eyes focused tightly on those two beautiful

pictures. No swastikas. No führer. No Blackshirts. No new and unpleasant rules. Just the smiling faces of well-fed children who were thinking about Christmas. There was the little girl with braids pinned on her head and the plump boy smiling as he spooned in the porridge. And there were the parents, smiling at each other as they served the humble fare in their finest porcelain.

More than anything, Egon was going to miss his family, the sure and certain knowledge that a short train ride in any direction were people who loved him, who would help him no matter what. As of tomorrow he was not going to have money, or a job, or even the ability to speak to anyone on the street. Far more important, he would be completely cut off from humanity. Starting tomorrow, he wouldn't know a blessed soul. Except for Heinz.

Another quick glance.

The men weren't chatting any longer. They ground their cigarette ends with their boot heels, and stiffened as they looked expectantly at the entrance.

No longer feigning interest in newspapers, Egon stared openly. The cars, the busy shoppers, the clanking of the trolley, all of it disappeared as Egon focused on the scene across the street.

Another Blackshirt joined them. Egon noticed the extra stripes on the man's shoulder. Their rifles were no longer slung casually, but gripped tightly, ready to be aimed.

No one else appeared to notice.

Notice what?

Suddenly the door burst open. There were two officers escorting a prisoner. No, not escorting—dragging.

Recognition battled with fear in Egon's consciousness. One of the men punched the prisoner in the stomach.

Egon grimaced. He couldn't take in the scene all at once. It was too terrifying.

Every instinct screamed at Egon to run. But he did not run. Reacting impulsively was what had gotten him into trouble in the first place. Egon closed his eyes for a moment. I will not pull out in front of the speeding car. I will not give them an excuse to come after me.

Instead of thinking, instead of yelling, instead of running, Egon focused on the unusual puffiness about Heinz's mouth, the narrow trickle of blood coming from his left eyebrow.

Egon flinched as another blow slammed into his friend's jaw. Another to the abdomen.

The men were laughing and joking again.

"Hey, you!" The voice was harsh.

Egon froze as he realized that the sound was directed at him.

24

"ou going to pay for that paper, or you going to stand there and wipe your ass with it?"

Struggling for control, Egon counted out a few coins and walked away. He forced himself to blend in with the holiday shoppers, to put one foot in front of the other at a moderate pace, to arrange his features into a mask of blankness.

As if for the first time, he noticed the viciousness of the rally posters pasted on every wall: JEWS NOT WELCOME. He noticed the sign at the movie house: JEWS, NO ADMISSION.

When he came to a red light, Egon felt his body might fly out of its skin. Standing still, doing nothing, even for a minute, was entirely beyond his ability.

Egon leaned against a lamppost and opened the newspaper in front of his face. He read the advertisements, the timetable for church services, and the "Holiday Helper" column about how to bake a cake very like his mother's holiday *butterkuchen*.

He was just about to close the paper when he was slammed in the face by a small article on page thirteen.

Police are searching for one Egon Katz, seventeen, who tied up his master baker in order to flee a rightful arrest warrant for violation of the Nuremberg Laws. He was the cause of a severe automobile accident earlier this month. Katz was last seen in Bremen, but some reports have put him near the Dutch border.

Like all Jews, Katz is devious and had obviously been plotting to leave the country illegally. He is also quick-tempered and violent. Neighbors still talk about the time he threw a superior through a window.

Katz is five feet six inches tall, blue eyes, brown hair, 145 pounds, and should be considered dangerous.

It was all he had feared and then some.

They would certainly go to Barntrup and interrogate his mother. Maybe they already had. The thought filled him with utter helplessness. Bad as that was, however, his next thought was worse.

If they'd found Heinz, they would find him too.

Egon had been afraid before, even terrified as he slipped away from the bakery in the shadow of the Blackshirts, but never before had he felt utter panic.

"I WOULD SAY"—Bruno pointed at the newspaper squib—"that no one could possibly recognize you from this."

"But they're looking for me, Bruno."

"They're not looking for *you*. They're looking for some thug." Bruno snapped the newspaper with his hand. " '. . . tied up his master baker . . . threw a superior through a window.' Where do they get this?"

Egon shifted in his seat.

Bruno glanced at him, alert.

"I never tied anyone up." Egon looked away. "The baker wasn't even there when I left."

Bruno waited.

Egon chewed his cuticles.

"And the window?"

"I didn't throw anyone through the window." His finger was bleeding now.

"So what happened?"

"I just got so tired of taking orders. . . ." Egon began talking fast. "You don't know what it's like. Up at two-thirty in the morning. Never enough sleep. Being ordered around constantly. 'Fetch this . . . do that . . . clean the other . . . go help Mrs. So-and-so. . . .' And if you don't move fast enough, the yelling gets louder, with names and curses thrown in, and you can't go to sleep early because the walls are so thin, and every day it's up again at two-thirty in the morning."

Bruno waited.

Egon sighed. "It was in the fall, around the High Holidays. Herman Levi brought in two journeymen bakers to deal with the holiday rush. One of them was all right, but the other . . ." Egon shivered. "Rudy Mendelbaum. He had just gotten his journeyman certificate and was gleeful about finally having someone to order around. He'd wait until I was in the middle of a job, then yell at me to fill the lemon tarts, check the macaroons, sharpen the knives. He liked to stand and watch while I scurried around like some dizzy children's puppet.

"One morning I slapped him."

The brothers stared at each other.

"And?"

"Rudy Mendelbaum tossed me through the front window."

"*He* threw *you*?"

Egon nodded. "I didn't mention that Rudy Mendelbaum is the size of an overfed Goliath."

"You get hurt?"

Egon shrugged. "The doctor spent an hour picking glass out of my arms. I went back to work the next day."

Bruno folded the newspaper and threw it onto the floor.

At the time the incident had seemed so horrible. Egon could still feel the glass shattering around his ears, the instinct that had brought his arms in front of his face, the sharp pain of a thousand needles, the gaping silence as he lay on the cement, wondering how to protect himself from whatever Rudy Mendelbaum thought of next.

At least then it was an in-the-flesh enemy who stood before him.

The present, however, lapped up around Egon's chin, demanding his full attention.

"They're beating up Heinz," he said. "They probably already know about Sweden. Soon they'll know about the warrant. Everything."

"So we make another plan. . . ." Bruno paused. "Get you out of here right now. Today."

Again the maps. Again the train and bus schedules.

Suddenly Bruno looked up, assumed his schoolteacher voice. "Egon, you simply cannot lose your temper. If you slap anyone now, they will shoot you dead. If you smile at a pretty girl, you will go to prison. And you'd better remember that, because no one is going to be there to bail you out."

"Yes. Yes." Egon waved the concern away. "Bruno, they could be here any minute."

Bruno turned again to the map, using his index finger as a pointer. "Don't flatter yourself, little brother. The whole Reich is not out looking for you."

"But we're so easy to find. You're in danger too."

Bruno shook his head. "Heinz doesn't know where I live. And if they call the school to find out . . . well . . . they certainly can't expect any information today, on the Sabbath." He smiled. "Or Christmas Eve, depending on how you look at it."

Was Bruno's optimism warranted? Egon didn't know, but it was all he had.

"So, how do you feel about Denmark?"

"Denmark?"

"Uh-huh." Bruno looked up from the map. "It's not so far away. And there's a Jewish community in Copenhagen."

"What about the border?"

"That's the beautiful thing about Denmark." Bruno became more animated. "If you'd paid more attention in history class, you'd know that the German-Danish border area has been disputed for generations. The actual border has been shifted several times. A lot of Germans live in southern Denmark. That should make it easier for you."

Denmark. Egon rolled the idea around in his mind. All he knew about Denmark was one word: Vikings. There was still the language problem. And the lack of a lifeline on the other side. . . .

"Denmark sounds fine."

They turned back to the map, examining every dot and dash of the border. Bruno spoke softly, as if thinking aloud. "Flensburg is the border city, an obvious but well-patrolled choice. If it were me, I'd rather cross at a small town."

"Small town is good."

Together they examined each small town in the border region.

"How about Ellund." Egon was startled at his own initiative.

Bruno nodded. "You can ride the bus to Ellund, which looks to be only a mile and a half from the border."

"Then I'll just walk across to Tinglev."

Bruno nodded.

"And if it doesn't look good right there, I'll just dodge about the countryside and walk across the border with some cows."

"Now you're thinking."

Bruno fixed Egon a sandwich for the bus ride.

The less they dwelled on the plan, the less noticeable its weaknesses. If Egon really sat and imagined what it would be like to walk across the border past German rifles, to make his way alone to Copenhagen—to sleep . . . where? to eat . . . what?—it would be too much. He would be too terrified to leave.

But he had to leave. He would have to do all those things, soon enough. He didn't have to think about them now.

Instead of crying, they laughed. Egon teased Bruno about Sabina. Bruno told Egon that they'd know he was safe, "because we'll be able to hear you snoring all the way from Copenhagen."

"And I'll hear your students moan when you walk into class each morning."

With the exception of his mother, Egon was closer to Bruno than to anyone else in the family. He and Bruno had gone on berry-picking and rock-throwing expeditions together. They'd spent hours tending animals for their father. And they'd slept in the same bed for years. So it was possible Bruno was even right about the snoring.

"Sure you won't come with me?"

Bruno looked down.

"She must be a very special girl." Sabina was to have come over that evening and lit the Hanukkah candles with them.

"Very special."

Soon, though, it would be time for Egon to leave. Bruno gave Egon his best suit. "Remember, you're visiting family for the holiday, and we want you to look presentable."

Egon looked longingly at the hem of his rumpled old coat before putting on Bruno's crisp overcoat. "Send the money to Mama, will you?"

"Sure."

Egon thrust his hands into the pockets. This time there was no reassuring slip of paper. No spare clothes. No money. No Mr. Ritter. No Heinz.

This time was for keeps.

25

When the bus reached the end of the line, just outside Ellund, there were only three remaining passengers, Egon and two local women laden with Christmas bundles.

As Egon got off the bus, he was struck by the beauty of the place. He'd spent too much time in the city. It was easy to forget how beautiful a country winter scene could be. The village was a quarter mile away, and the small sturdy houses in the snowy landscape looked inviting, smoke from the chimneys promising warmth that contrasted with the numbing cold outside.

Damn.

As he walked casually behind the two women, his eyes were assaulted by the sight, a hundred yards away, of a uniformed German guard. At least he was only wearing brown, but even at this distance Egon could see the shine on the black rifle barrel.

If there was a guard all the way out here at the entrance to the border zone—over a mile from the actual border— he and Bruno had vastly underestimated security. There would certainly be a much more elaborate setup at the actual crossing point. But he couldn't worry about that yet. What was he going to tell the guard here?

With every step, the man—and his rifle—became more defined.

Egon's fears doubled. He was a terrible liar. He had always tried to behave well at home and school, not because he found the straight and narrow so appealing, but because he feared the consequences—the sting of his father's belt and the hurt look in his mother's eyes—if he didn't. And now the consequences had increased tenfold. Unbidden, the image of Heinz Rosenthal, bruised and battered, came to mind. The thought of Leni, vanished without a trace, hovered over him.

In just a few minutes he, too, could be hustled away, and no one would ever know what happened to him.

The instinct that had brought Egon's arms to his face as he was hurled through the glass now told him to turn around, to run, to shroud himself in anonymity.

The anger that had made him slap Rudy Mendelbaum made Egon see the guard not as an obstacle, but a target. If he could just get the gun away, he would do what had been done to him, and then some.

In that brief moment, as he teetered between anger and instinct, Egon grasped at an idea. There was no time to deliberate.

He quickened his pace, bringing into ever sharper focus the outlines of the guard's boots, the long, heavy coat that obscured his body.

He was closing in on them.

Soon. A few more steps. It would have to be now, or the guard might hear.

"Good afternoon, ladies," Egon called.

The women stopped and turned around.

He made his voice even more friendly. "Merry Christmas."

They smiled. "Merry Christmas."

"You certainly have a lovely town here."

"Thank you." It was the older, heavier one who spoke.

Egon was relieved that they were cheerful and apparently not the least bit suspicious.

He thought of the most common nickname he could.

"My friend Heini always told me how nice Ellund was, that I should come and visit—we worked together in Flensburg, you know." Although the pace had slowed considerably, they had resumed walking. "Anyway, Heini finally invites me, for Christmas dinner no less, and forgets to give me directions. Does either of you happen to know where he lives?"

Please. Please.

"Heini?"

"You mean Heini Gertsner?" This time it was the younger one. "He was a locksmith's apprentice in Flensburg."

"Yes, that's him."

"Sure. He lives over the locksmith's shop. Turn left at the main street up ahead; you can't miss it."

"Thanks very much." Egon had to restrain himself from giving her a hug. Instead, he slowed his pace, allowing the women to get ahead of him.

A dozen more steps, and they would be even with the guard.

The women obviously had familiar faces. The guard simply exchanged waves with them.

Egon was next.

He turned up his collar, hoping to partially obscure his delicate face, to look as little as possible like anyone who might be wanted by the Gestapo.

"Who are you?" The voice was stiff. "And where are you going?"

Egon was careful to omit his name. "I'm visiting my friend Heini Gertsner." He did his best to sound casual. "My brother was a locksmith in Flensburg with Heini, and I am a baker." No lie in the latter part, anyway.

"That's right. Heini's a good man. *Heil* Hitler."

"*Heil* Hitler."

Euphoria almost instantly gave way to a feeling of, what now?

More than anything Egon wanted to keep walking north, to somehow get across the border—not in three days, not tomorrow—*now*. It was, however, still full light, and if Egon kept on heading north, the guard would have ample opportunity to use the rifle he held so conspicuously.

Instead, Egon turned left into Ellund. He decided to go say hello to his old friend Heini Gertsner.

26

U p close the buildings were not quaint, but in desperate need of repair. The snow was pockmarked and gray. The cold, which before had been kept at bay by fear, now stung Egon's cheeks and glided in between the buttonholes of Bruno's coat.

The locksmith's shop was across the street, between the inn and the butcher.

Egon observed from where he stood. The young man inside looked to be in his early twenties. Business everywhere was clearly winding down, and Heini Gertsner was tidying up. No one was going to need the services of a locksmith this afternoon. Why not just close up shop? Immediately Egon knew the answer. The shop was not Heini's to close. He was a journeyman, as much under the thumb of his master as Egon had been under Herman Levi's.

Avoiding the slushy puddles, Egon crossed the narrow street.

He stared through the window. No Christmas decorations here. But no swastikas either. The man reminded Egon of someone.

The dim light inside washed away color, but the deliberateness of the man's motions was easy to see. He straightened a stack of papers on the counter and then reached for a pencil. The precision of his figuring reminded Egon of Bruno. Yes, Bruno—that's who he looked like. Not the size, certainly, and the stance was off, but the face was definitely familiar.

Egon knew that, in order to make it across the border, he was going to have to trust someone. Heini Gertsner was as good as any.

There had to be some casual way to bring up the subject.

I'm just passing through.

True.

Heading toward Tinglev.

Also true.

My friends in Tinglev neglected to mention whether I'd need documents at the border.

A stretch, but it might work. It had to work.

Egon opened the door.

Heini Gertsner, who had not noticed him before, looked up.

Despite the journeyman's tidying, everything in the store was covered with a film of dust and grime.

"Good afternoon," said Egon.

"Can I help you with something?" The voice was utterly neutral.

"I'm not sure yet."

Heini laughed. "Let me know when you find out."

"You see, I'm just passing through—" Just as he was about to crash through the glass, Egon's arms shot up to protect his face.

The guard had called Heini "a good man." What were the chances that Egon and that guard would ever agree in their definition of "a good man"?

On closer inspection, Heini Gertsner didn't look at all

118

like Bruno. They had the same coloring, but Heini's expectant face was overly wide and doughy.

Heini waited for Egon to continue. There was no obvious reason not to—Egon was dressed for traveling; he *could* be visiting friends in Tinglev—but still he didn't speak. Instead, he listened.

You have good instincts—Sam's words came through just as clearly as they had that night in the attic—*be careful whom you trust.*

It was then that Egon noticed the party handbills stacked on the counter.

"So you're passing through," said Heini. "Perhaps you need a lock for your journey."

"No." Egon cleared his throat. "Actually, I am looking for the inn."

"The inn?"

"Yes."

"Leave your glasses at home?"

Now Egon was both frightened and confused. What was the man talking about, glasses? Maybe it was some sort of code. He needed to get out of here, fast, without calling any more attention to himself. Something he had said had obviously been misinterpreted. Egon tried to undo the damage.

"Sorry to have bothered you, Mr. Gertsner. I'll just—"

"How do you know my name?" Now his tone was accusatory.

Egon stepped backward. Instead of mitigating the damage, he had compounded it. Think fast. How do I know his name?

"A couple of attractive girls on the bus were talking about you." Egon forced a smile. "It was a *very* intriguing conversation."

"Really?" Heini was suddenly interested. "What did they have to say?"

Egon tried to sound conspiratorial. "All favorable, I assure you."

Heini nodded and smiled. "The inn's right next door."

27

Egon stared dully at his cooling coffee. Out of one frying pan and into another. So far the innkeeper hadn't said anything, but then, he didn't have to. The swastika blazing from his jacket came through clear and loud.

The man was middle-aged and had obviously partaken of plenty of the beer he poured out for the rowdy customers. "We're the smart ones," Egon heard one of them say. "Everyone else is in church." There was singing and cheerful voices, and the smell of good food. Merrymaking was wasted on him, however, even if he had been included. Which he was not.

He could think of nothing beyond the present, and the innkeeper's eyes, which looked over at him every few moments. The eyes did not seem unkind, or suspicious, but they were curious. Everyone else in this room had grown up together. Egon did not belong. The happy customers might be too busy to notice him, but the innkeeper was obviously interested.

"Another coffee?" he asked.

"No, thank you."

"How about some food?"

"No, thanks."

Still the man stood by the corner table, staring at Egon. "Are you here to look at the new road?"

Egon didn't answer. Instead he stared at the man, taking his measure. The swastika was probably just an expression of national pride. The man knew Egon didn't belong here, but was merely inquisitive, not hostile.

No, I'm not here to look at the road. I'm trying to escape the Gestapo. Will you help me? Saying the words was impossible. Saying nothing was equally impossible. The man had asked him a direct question. Egon cast about for an innocuous reply.

"Your local history lessons must be quite complicated," he said.

The innkeeper nodded. "We have always been the rope in the tug-of-war between Copenhagen and Berlin."

"So you speak Danish?"

"Naturally." The reply, in Danish, was readily understandable to Egon. He leaned against the wall. Apparently the innkeeper was bored with pulling beers. Conversation with an outsider was much more diverting, even if the question about the road had been ignored. They chatted for several minutes before Egon meandered delicately toward the point.

"So there are ethnic Danes who live here, and Germans who live on the other side?"

"Certainly. On the map a border seems concrete. Absolute. But living here, it's obvious that a border is entirely political. Artificial. They don't affect feelings."

Egon was encouraged. "Still, it must be very difficult when a border is shoved around like this one has been."

"Extremely difficult." The man nodded. "The border doesn't affect how you feel. But it has an enormous impact on everything else. Where you work, what language you speak, how freely you travel, your military obligations, taxes . . . everything.''

''What about the human consequences?''

''That more than anything. Families have been split up over it.'' For a long time he stared without seeing. Finally he turned his head away. ''My own brother lives in Denmark. I haven't seen him in ten years.''

The silence broadened and deepened as the man appeared to be remembering long-ago Christmas Eves with his estranged brother, and Egon considered the most important decision of his life.

You have good instincts.

Past and future evaporated into this one moment. Egon cleared his throat and spoke quietly. ''I'm not here about the new road.'' One more word and there would be no going back. ''I'm a baker's apprentice from Bremen.'' A slight hesitation. ''A Jewish baker's apprentice.''

The innkeeper looked directly at him.

''My scooter was hit. It's a long story, but I have to get out of Germany. Tonight.''

The man shook his head slightly, then rubbed the back of his neck. He touched Egon on the shoulder. ''I'll be right back.''

Egon watched intently as the innkeeper pulled more beers for his regular customers. Was he going to contact the authorities? Egon watched his every move. A shake of the head. A rub on the neck. A touch on the shoulder. What did that add up to?

He could run, but where?

Finally the innkeeper returned to the table with a fresh cup of coffee. ''On the house.'' He sat down next to Egon.

Egon allowed himself a small sigh of relief. Clearly the man wasn't going to turn him in. But neither did a cup of coffee necessarily mean anything more. Egon would have to let the man speak first. The wait was not as long as it seemed.

His voice was low. "I am a member of the party." He nodded toward the swastika on his jacket. "But what they are doing to you people is wrong."

Instincts confirmed, Egon rushed to the point. "What sort of control is there at the border?"

"Don't even think about crossing there."

"Where then?"

Egon could watch the man weighing alternatives.

"You can't do anything in daylight."

Egon glanced outside at the lengthening shadows. Hard to believe he had come so far—and still had so far to go—in one day.

The innkeeper spoke in a whisper. "Cross the street and make the first turn to the right. That road will dwindle away pretty quickly, but keep going a little ways and you'll see my barn.

"Hide behind the barn until it's completely dark. The border is one kilometer straight north from the fence line. Once you get across the pasture, it's heavily wooded, so no one will see you."

That's all there was to it? All this way, hiding in rooms, studying maps, fearing for his life, and he was going to simply go for a walk in the woods? It sounded too good to be true.

"I thank you," said Egon. "And my mother thanks you."

28

gon paced behind the barn. It was full dark now. He was sure of his bearings. North was straight ahead. The snow was a foot deep. One of the few clouds had passed in front of the nearly full moon. The only barriers were pasture fences.

A lonely bird squawked at him once. Other than that, there was utter silence.

Still Egon hesitated. It was one thing to joke

. . . with Bruno

. . . in daylight

. . . in Hamburg

. . . about walking across the border.

It was another matter altogether to stand

. . . here

. . . alone

. . . in the dark

. . . at the edge of the precipice.

A large part of him was exhilarated at the thought of finally being free. A larger part of him was terrified. This time he had no one. Even though it was dark, as he walked across the pasture he would be a clear target. He would leave tracks. There would be no more opportunity for fictions about visiting friends for dinner.

Egon held the strands of barbed wire apart and eased his way through.

A day or two old, the snow was crisp on top and soft underneath. Egon had to lift his knees with every step. It was cold, wet going. He tried to walk quickly, to step higher, to breathe deeper, partly to get across the pasture more quickly, partly to keep his feet from going numb.

Halfway across the broad field, exhaustion and fear battled for control of his senses.

Right. Left. Breathe.

His internal tension magnified every sensation—the cold, the dark, the wet.

Inside his city gloves Egon flexed his fingers awake. He had to keep his hands out of his pockets because he needed them for balance.

Three-quarters of the way across. Once he got into the woods, it would get easier. The tree branches would have caught the snow, and at least he wouldn't have that to deal with.

Right. Left. Breathe.

Egon checked his bearings to make sure he was still headed due north.

Only a few more steps now.

He stood still, breathing heavily as he rested a moment before climbing through the fence.

"Damn."

The barbed wire ripped Bruno's coat across the shoulder. But there was no time to worry about that now.

The temperature continued to drop, yet, even with the gaping hole in his coat, Egon didn't notice it. Every step was bringing him closer to Danish soil. No one could see him here. And as he had predicted, there was no snow beneath the trees. But he had not anticipated a path. An actual path!

Despite the exhaustion, Egon wanted to skip. He hadn't skipped in years. The innkeeper had said one kilometer north of the barn. A kilometer was hardly any distance at all, a ten-minute walk. Certainly more with the snow and all, but it was at least half an hour since he'd left the barn.

Any moment now. The border could be here, or here, or here. With each step his smile grew. All alone, and he was doing it. He had done it, surely! Surely by now. There was no welcome banner. The evergreen trees didn't change, nor did the temperature, but they might as well have.

With every step he was becoming safer. The future was still uncertain. It was the future he had escaped that was certain.

Another ten minutes. Egon took to patting the trees— Danish trees—as he passed. The smiles and grins and the occasional skip could no longer express his happiness.

And so he began to sing. He sang the children's songs he had wanted to sing on the train, the songs his mother and sisters used to sing to him, songs from a time when every story had a happy ending.

"Halt."

The language was German and the voice curt.

Suddenly frozen, Egon looked for the voice, but the speaker, he thought, must be hiding behind a tree.

"Where are you coming from?"

"Ellund."

"Where are you going?"

The voice seemed to come from everywhere. How many were there? *Where was he going?* Egon quickly weighed various answers. "I'm going to Tinglev."

"No you're not."

A guard appeared. At first Egon couldn't distinguish the man's uniform, but then, he didn't need to. His accent told Egon as well as any uniform that the guard was Danish, not German. Still, it was easy enough to make out the rifle pointed firmly at his chest.

The man stepped closer. "Turn around and march."

"Please." Egon stood his ground.

The momentary lack of response was encouraging. More encouraging was the fact that it was not a military, but a police uniform the man was wearing. Egon sorted through various appeals, and finally settled on the truth. "Please, I'm fleeing the Gestapo. I had a scooter accident, that's all. I'm a baker's apprentice, seventeen years old."

The man paused. "Jewish?"

"Yes."

Egon detected a slight shake of the head and breathed slightly easier as the man shifted the rifle to his shoulder. But he was doing something with his hands.

Pffft. He lit a cigarette.

"Would you like one?"

"No thanks." Egon tried to sound as casual as his captor. "How about if you let me go and tell your boss it was a dull night."

"Can't do that." The man smoked leisurely. "Don't blame you, though, for trying. The other day I had to take back a Jewish family. My German counterpart beat them, even the children, with his rifle butt right there at the border." The guard shivered as he took a long drag. "I'll never forget that."

Fear erupted in Egon's throat, seizing his very soul. "Please. No one would ever have to know."

"Don't worry." He shook his head. "I'm not going to

send you back. But I do have to take you to my superior. He'll decide what to do."

Egon nodded dully. Surely a Danish prison was preferable to a German one.

"Come on." The guard sounded almost cheerful. "Let's go."

They walked side by side, the guard smoking. As he chatted amiably, it occurred to Egon that this was a pleasant diversion for the young man. How many long, lonely nights had he spent patrolling those same woods? Still, Egon couldn't bring himself to care about the gift the guard had bought for his girlfriend, or the menu for their Christmas dinner—held off a day because of his work schedule.

The man acted as both tour guide and cheerleader. "Sergeant Thompson is a fair man; you'll see."

Egon answered in monosyllables and only when necessary. With every puff of the man's cigarette, with every twist of the path, he sought a chance to run.

It was hopeless. However casually held, the guard's rifle was not to be ignored. Equally important was the fact that it would be impossible to outrun or outmaneuver the man here, in his own territory. And if he tried, the man's obvious goodwill would surely disappear.

Besides, it was too late.

They were no longer walking along a path but were on a road. The woods gave way gradually to a small town.

The two young men walked side by side. The casual observer could not have guessed that Egon was a prisoner.

Egon nodded. He was numb, not with cold or fright—though there certainly was that—but with some horrible deadening sensation he had never before experienced. It was as if his body—or his mind—had created an entirely new plane of existence that would allow him to survive whatever was coming. Part of that new state was a complete absence of feelings. Hope, fear, anger, futility, rage, and a dozen more hovered, for now, well outside Egon's realm. For if he allowed himself the luxury, he would drown in emotion.

He no longer counted steps, or breaths. He no longer braced himself for the worst. He was simply a prisoner, strolling along as if this walk were the most natural thing in the world.

"Right around the corner."

The stone houses were closer together now. The snow had been shoveled from the walkway but lay in pristine squares in front of the cheerful homes. Egon stared at the houses. Was it his imagination, or were they vastly more beautiful than those on the other side? Warm yellow light spilled out of every window. There was music, and songs with words that Egon did not understand.

The guard led the way up a short walkway, then onto a raised stoop.

Knock. Knock. Knock.

If he was annoyed at being disturbed at home on Christmas Eve, Sergeant Thompson didn't show it.

Egon listened intently, but he couldn't understand a word of their rapid-fire Danish. Even the tone wasn't particularly helpful. The words, to Egon's ear, sounded business-like, purposeful. Since listening didn't help, Egon watched.

Sergeant Thompson was precise and elegant in his dress uniform, a crisper, more embellished version of the police uniform the guard wore. A tall, slender man, he looked to be about forty. His dark blond hair showed only the faintest trace of gray at the temple. His face was immaculately shaven and his eyes were an intense blue. After the briefest glance at Egon, Sergeant Thompson listened as the guard explained.

Suddenly the guard turned. "What's your name?"

Egon hesitated briefly. "Egon Katz."

The explanation continued. By concentrating fiercely, he was able to catch an occasional word that resembled the German—"baker," "Jewish"—but the effort was exhausting and mostly futile, since by the time Egon had translated the one word, the men had spoken several more incomprehensible sentences.

Suddenly Egon noticed a pretty blond head in the doorway.

"Go back inside."

That time Egon understood perfectly well, especially since the head disappeared immediately.

The guard waved casually as he turned to go.

"Welcome to Denmark, young man."

That Sergeant Thompson spoke German didn't surprise Egon. The words, however, were a shock, as was the broad smile that accompanied them.

29

Egon was even more encouraged when Sergeant Thompson ushered him inside, as if he were an invited guest.

The room was small, but beautiful. There was a spruce tree a-twinkle with small white candles. Danish flags, white cross on red background, decorated one wall. And there were brightly colored ribbons bearing the greeting GLADELID JUL. The cheery fireplace—wood-, not coal-burning—combined with the delicious smells of a holiday dinner to produce the most marvelous aroma. Although Egon could not honestly remember when he'd last experienced it, the smell of roast goose was distinctive and extremely pleasant. His mouth watered involuntarily.

"I'll need to call my superiors about you"—Sergeant Thompson spoke casually—"but I don't think there's anything to worry about."

Egon nodded, stunned both by the familial beauty of the place and the simple fact that he was here. The pretty blond girl, about his age, Egon guessed, stared at him from near the shoulder of an older version of the same face, almost certainly her mother.

"Papa?"

Sergeant Thompson made introductions in both Danish

and German. The woman was, of course, Mrs. Thompson; the girl was their daughter, Marrike.

Mrs. Thompson approached Egon to take his coat. She frowned as she noticed the gaping hole at the shoulder. She looked at him with a question mark, the same look his mother had had when he came home with holes at his knees.

How to explain barbed wire without words? Egon just shrugged.

No big deal? It was as if Egon could read Marrike's mind. *He escapes across the border, half frozen, coat torn to shreds, and he says it's no big deal.* She stared at him with even greater interest.

Sergeant Thompson brought Egon a cup of hot cider and escorted him to a chair beside the fire. Mrs. Thompson fetched a small sewing basket.

Egon stared in disbelief as she began repairing the rip.

The Thompsons spoke to one another. Then Mrs. Thompson said something to Marrike, and the girl disappeared into the kitchen.

Probably having her stir the soup, thought Egon. She returned a moment later and smiled shyly at Egon before laying another place at the table.

As his feet thawed, Egon felt that needles were being poked into his cold wet toes, but he didn't care.

Mrs. Thompson was *fixing his coat*.

They were *having him to dinner*.

Sergeant Thompson said *there was nothing to worry about*.

It was too much. Maybe he'd fallen asleep back in the woods and this was all a dream. Or he hadn't fallen asleep . . . he was still stumbling around, frozen in the woods, and this was a hallucination. Or wishful thinking.

But the chair was comfortable underneath him. The cup

was warm in his hands. The cider was sweet in his mouth. They were the most real sensations he had ever experienced.

Like warmth to his feet, Egon felt his entire consciousness returning to life. He had made it! He was out of Germany! He was wet and he was tired. But he was also free—and he was hungry. And he was happy. No. Happy wasn't a grand enough word. He was happy beyond words. Ecstatic. Delirious.

Egon smiled uncontrollably.

Marrike apparently thought his smile was directed at her. It was not such a terrible misunderstanding.

"We'll be eating soon," Sergeant Thompson said. "My wife thought you might like to use the washroom first."

"Thank you." Egon nodded at her as Sergeant Thompson led the way.

As he stood alone in the simple bathroom, Egon realized for the first time that his hosts—for that was how he thought of them—were not wealthy. It was not the luxury of velvet or crystal that thrilled him, but the even greater luxury of people who saw beyond politics, beyond religion, to a simple human being in trouble.

It was their warmth and kindness that lit up the room, that welcomed him.

Egon took stock of himself. He was wet from the knee down. From the waist up, however, he had come through unscathed. His clothes still looked presentable, almost sharp. Egon smiled. Apparently it had not been a lie at all. He *had* been headed to Tinglev to have Christmas dinner with friends.

When he returned, Sergeant Thompson was on the telephone. The conversation was obviously about Egon.

Sergeant Thompson spoke casually at first. Egon wasn't sure whether it was the tone of the man's voice or the expression on his face, but the exchange was obviously not going as expected.

Marrike and Mrs. Thompson stood, frozen except for their heads, which bounced back and forth like metronomes between Egon and Sergeant Thompson.

The call lasted no more than a few minutes, but the tighter Sergeant Thompson's face became, the longer the eternity lasted. He stared at Egon as he spoke into the receiver.

As Egon returned the stare, he felt his cheeks flush and his throat tighten. It was a vise of hopelessness now affecting his breathing and his vision.

He was going to cry.

No. Anger, determination, and pride rose up to save him from the humiliation. But the despair was too great. His eyes filled involuntarily.

Egon turned and walked away to lean against the wall. He heard Sergeant Thompson's angry Danish and he felt the woman's bewildered pity. He felt helpless. Hopeless.

The silence was overwhelming.

"I'm sorry, Egon, but my orders are to take you back to the German border."

Back to the border. It was what he feared most of all. If he had to go to prison, couldn't it be a Danish prison? Was he, like Leni, going to simply disappear forever? A beating he could survive, but to simply vanish into a bleak pit of the unknown . . . for his family to speak of him in the past tense . . . he might as well be dead.

Egon's misery exceeded tears. Suddenly he didn't care anymore. About anything. Every time he allowed himself to care, to believe that maybe he would make it, an impossible barrier appeared in front of his face.

There were hands on his shoulders. Marrike and Mrs.

Thompson shepherded him from the corner to his place at the table, both of them scowling toward Sergeant Thompson all the while. He raised his palms in a gesture of futility.

But that wasn't good enough for the women, who lit into the man with verbal attacks.

Egon imagined what they were saying.

"It's Christmas. How can you possibly send him back?"

"Are you going to stand there and watch while the Germans beat him up?"

Shoulders slumping, Sergeant Thompson endured the punishment, for a time. Three angry syllables from him, however, and all was quiet.

THE MEAL WAS ROAST GOOSE, ALL RIGHT. The skin was brown and crispy. The serving platters for the side dishes would hardly fit on the small table. If Egon squinted, he could imagine the candles on either side of the roast were Hanukkah candles. But for tonight there should be seven.

A word from Mrs. Thompson, and suddenly Egon realized that Sergeant Thompson was saying a prayer.

To himself, Egon repeated the blessing over the Hanukkah candles. It didn't do any good. Enough oil for one night had supposedly burned, instead, for eight. A baby boy was born in a stable. For hundreds, thousands, of years people had been commemorating these supposed miracles, organizing calendars around them, lighting candles for them, and, most important, being inspired by them. And all that praying, lighting, and inspiring hadn't helped a bit.

As the last sounds of the prayer faded away, the table returned to stony silence, broken only by the soft clink of serving utensils.

Mrs. Thompson carved, then served Egon first.

He would never be able to eat the huge portion on his

plate, but he nodded and managed a faint smile for Mrs. Thompson.

When she saw him passing over the other dishes, she took charge completely, staring sternly at her husband between heaping scoops.

The food had been lovingly prepared, but Egon ate only a little, and that mechanically, without tasting.

The silence deepened as the Thompsons exchanged glares.

But when Egon glanced across the table, Marrike was smiling at him. Instantly Egon looked at his plate. He was not going to cry again, especially not in front of the girl.

Over and over again he poked his fork into his apple fritter. The prospects were too gloomy to think of, too terrifying and close at hand to avoid thinking of.

Perhaps if he weren't sitting here at their dinner table, it wouldn't be so bad. The Thompsons were clearly good people. Mrs. Thompson hadn't hesitated. When she saw his coat was torn, she fixed it for him. Sergeant Thompson had greeted him with a smile. *Welcome to Denmark.* Marrike obviously saw him as she might any other boy. He was a stranger. It was Christmas Eve. There was no question of whether he would eat with them.

And now?

The Thompsons, he supposed, were still good people. One telephone call obviously hadn't changed that, but it had forced all four of them firmly into assigned roles.

Egon was no longer merely a wayward traveler. He was now a German Jew who had crossed the border illegally and had to be dealt with accordingly.

Marrike and Mrs. Thompson no longer saw him as someone to be helped, but someone to be pitied.

And Sergeant Thompson? His livelihood depended on enforcing the law, no matter how unpleasant that might be.

How could four people be so effectively forced into roles that contradicted their natures? For perhaps the hundredth time in the past three weeks, Egon wished that he had paid more attention. Read more newspapers. Studied harder at school. Paid better attention at synagogue. Perhaps then he would be able to understand.

He knew that Denmark desperately wanted to remain free of German influence, but why should either Denmark or Germany care in the least about one baker boy? It was clearly and absolutely beyond Egon's ability to comprehend.

His feet were wet. The initial relief at getting them warmed had long since passed. Now they were simply wet and uncomfortable. He had stopped even pretending to eat.

After the painful silence, the sound of a voice, any voice was startling. And Marrike's voice was startlingly beautiful.

Egon couldn't understand the words, of course, but sensed that she spoke simply and eloquently.

Her father's reply was a sad shake of the head.

Again Marrike spoke. This time her sentences were longer; her appeal, though insistent, was still clearly within the bounds of daughterly propriety.

Again Sergeant Thompson shook his head.

Now Mrs. Thompson joined in.

Egon sat, stunned and silent, as they discussed him. He couldn't follow a word, so he constructed a conversation for himself.

"But Papa, you can't just send him back."

"I have orders, direct orders, to do exactly that."

"But they'll beat him up, or shoot him, or send him to one of those awful camps."

"You want me to lose my job over this boy?"

Egon watched Mrs. Thompson. Her tone was even. *"After you take him back, what will happen to him?"*

"I don't know."

She glanced over at Egon, then back at her husband. *"He certainly doesn't look very dangerous."*

"Papa, he's the same age as me. What if they wanted you to send me off somewhere and you didn't know what was going to happen to me?"

"No one is going to ask a father to turn in his daughter."

"But he hasn't done anything wrong."

"We don't know that."

"But if it was me, you'd check first. You'd make sure."

"It's not you, Marrike. There are thousands and thousands of people just like him. I cannot risk our family because this boy stumbled into our home tonight."

No matter how he manipulated the argument, Egon could not make the decision come out in his favor. Still, the discussion continued, with Marrike and Mrs. Thompson suggesting and Sergeant Thompson rejecting—not angrily, but nonetheless, clearly and explicitly rejecting.

Egon hoped that they were more creative than he had been. It gave him a peculiar feeling, being the cause of a major family argument but utterly unable to participate in the conversation on his own behalf.

Suddenly Sergeant Thompson slapped the table.

Egon recoiled, sure that the gesture was his final word on the matter. But no. While the argument was obviously over, Sergeant Thompson's craggy face had broken into a big grin. Egon glanced around the table, and the women, too, were smiling.

At him.

30

Egon was confused. A decision had obviously been made, and he had absolutely no idea what it was. He kept waiting for some sort of explanation, but it simply didn't come. The shy smiles and winks from Marrike were encouraging, but he needed more than that.

"Excuse me, sir," Egon said, "is there something that I should know?"

"Don't you worry." Sergeant Thompson placed a friendly hand on Egon's arm. "Let's forget about the whole Nazi business for a while and enjoy the rest of Mrs. Thompson's delicious dinner."

He had no alternative but to trust them.

The food tasted better now.

Mrs. Thompson didn't even ask, simply heaped his plate with seconds. And Egon ate that too. He was hungry, yes, but the food was also a comfort, proof of the goodwill they felt for him.

Sergeant Thompson had said not to worry, and so, for the moment, Egon would do his best. It was impossible to eat and worry at the same time. So Egon ate. More potatoes and pickles. More goose. More rolls with butter.

Finally Egon set down his cutlery, handles together at

the four o'clock position to indicate that he was finished, for he could eat no more.

Sergeant Thompson said cheerfully, "Now we have dessert."

Egon moaned softly.

They all laughed at him.

Egon laughed back. It was nice to be able to communicate without words. "Seriously, sir, I don't mean to be impolite, but I cannot eat anoth—"

"But Marrike made it herself." The sergeant paused. "I'm sure she will be very disappointed if you don't at least try it."

Marrike stared at Egon expectantly.

"A little." Egon placed his thumb and index finger close together.

She smiled and nodded.

The women left and returned a minute later with more dishes and coffee.

As Mrs. Thompson poured, Marrike stood nervously, holding her dessert.

Egon stared at her clear blue eyes and her perfect skin. She was younger than he had thought at first—physically a woman, but still awkward and unsure of herself in her new body. Probably fourteen or fifteen. Perhaps no more than thirteen. She had none of the self-assurance, the inner competence of a Katarina. But then, Egon told himself, she didn't have to. Marrike Thompson was the protected only child of secure parents. What a luxury. Maybe she really was seventeen but had simply never been forced to grow up.

"Go ahead." Sergeant Thompson nodded at his daughter.

Marrike kept rocking back and forth as she took a deep breath. "Is this I made *risengrod*?"

Egon smiled at her schoolgirl German.

Marrike's rocking speeded up. "*Risengrod* a special Christmas is. . . ." Flustered, she sat down and shook her head.

Egon spoke very slowly. "I'm sure it's very good." He looked at his host. "Please tell your daughter that her German is much better than my Danish."

Sergeant Thompson translated, and there were smiles all around.

As Marrike slowly and carefully served her creation, the sergeant completed the explanation for her. "*Risengrod*, or rice pudding, is a traditional Danish dish for Christmas Eve. Usually it is eaten as an appetizer, but my mother always served it as a dessert, and we're upholding that tradition."

Egon lifted his spoon. It was a simple rice pudding. He looked at Marrike. "It's very good."

"Thank you." Marrike smiled down at her own plate and played with her straight blond hair.

Fifteen at the most, Egon thought.

Suddenly she urged her father on.

"I forgot the important part. As you can tell, the *risengrod* has a smooth, somewhat ricey texture. But the cook hides one whole almond inside. The person who finds the almond is supposed to keep it a secret until everyone is finished."

"Why?"

"To keep everyone else from being disappointed. Whoever finds it gets a small prize: a piece of marzipan." He paused. "And more important, the finder of the almond has good luck for all of next year."

Egon nodded absently as he stirred his pudding. Such things were usually rigged. There was the nut, tucked into the corner of his dish. A whole year of good luck.

Would that it were so.

31

I t was time.

There was a sandwich in Egon's pocket. There was a pair of Sergeant Thompson's dry socks on his feet. Egon's newly repaired coat was on his shoulders. His stomach was full and his bladder was empty. Egon looked one more time at the comfortable living room.

Sergeant Thompson wore his pistol and his overcoat. They were leaving together. And Egon had absolutely no idea of their destination. He simply had to trust the man.

Trust was not Egon's strong point. He had trusted Mr. Ritter. He had trusted Heinz—and look what had happened to Heinz.

A last wave for Marrike and Mrs. Thompson, and they were on their way into the darkness. To some sort of safe house? A train station? The possibilities seemed very limited, especially once Egon realized that they were headed south.

"Where are we going?"

"Sh. Patience." Sergeant Thompson put a finger to his lips.

A moment later, one of the few other people on the street called out to them.

"Merry Christmas, Sergeant Thompson."

"And a merry Christmas to you, Kristof."

As the men paused there on the sidewalk, Egon was very aware of the stranger's questioning eyes darting frequently in his direction. Sergeant Thompson surely noticed it, too, but didn't acknowledge it, and instead brought the conversation to a quick, though graceful, conclusion.

Too soon they were on their way again.

With increasing panic, Egon stared up at the cold, cloudless sky. Although it was not the precise direction he had come from early this evening, there was no question at all that they were headed due south, directly toward the German border.

Suddenly Egon remembered the pistol on Sergeant Thompson's belt. It was concealed, for the moment, under his coat, but its presence was a clear reminder of the man's position.

There was no chain, no visible demonstration of authority, but still—no matter how hospitable the Thompsons had been—Egon was a prisoner. A prisoner who was being marched slowly but surely south.

Egon's mind spun. It had been Marrike and Mrs. Thompson who argued on his behalf. Whatever the plan, Sergeant Thompson had agreed to it only reluctantly. Perhaps he simply wanted to pacify his wife and daughter. Perhaps he was really planning personally to hand Egon over to the border guards. Or worse yet, use that pistol.

But that was ridiculous. Would he have treated Egon so warmly if he planned such a cruel betrayal?

In an instant, all of Egon's fears were obliterated by one that was far worse—something Egon had hoped never to see again as long as he lived.

Blackshirts.

Three of them, walking firmly toward him and Sergeant Thompson.

Even in heavy coats, they were obvious.

Would the sergeant simply hand him over? Be done with him, here and now?

"Merry Christmas." It was the center one. He was not much taller, or much older, than Egon, but he clearly spoke for the other two.

"Evening." Sergeant Thompson was neutral. He—and Egon—stopped in the center of the walkway, forcing the Blackshirts to do the same.

Egon, a mouse in the sight of three hawks, worked to stay invisible in his coat. A wrong word, the slightest mistake, and it would all be over.

"What are you *boys* doing here?" Sergeant Thompson apparently was no happier with this meeting than Egon was.

"Just a little sightseeing in your fair town." Still the center one.

"I assume you brought authorization papers?"

"Why should we need authorization papers to visit our Danish friends?"

"Your friends are on the other side of the border."

They had broken the law and they knew it. The two on either side looked ready to bolt. It was the first time Egon had ever seen Blackshirts look uncomfortable.

"We have friends everywhere." The center voice was firm. "Also enemies everywhere."

Egon's remaining fear vaporized in an explosion of rage. They were so close he could slap them.

They were monsters, acting without pity or humanity.

With only a slight squint, Egon could see the three of them beating up Heinz in front of the apartment building.

He could see them pounding on the bakery door, frightening Mrs. Levi to death. He could see them brandishing his arrest warrant. He could see them throwing a brick through his mother's window. He could see them hustling Bruno off to prison. And he could plainly see them intercepting Leni as she got off the train, brushing their hands against her cheek before leading her off into the dark unknown.

Sightseeing. Ha!

Egon was strong. He would be able to kill one of them, perhaps two, before he was stopped. Two less Blackshirts in the world. It would be worth it.

There was no delay between thought and action. His strong right hand tightened into a fist. No calluses, perhaps, but he'd been kneading bread, quietly building his strength, waiting for years for this moment.

He focused on the face of the center one. Before they could react, he pulled back his hand.

Snap.

Sergeant Thompson was faster. He grabbed Egon's wrist and held him tight and still.

Had they even noticed?

"I think"—Sergeant Thompson's voice was colder than the temperature—"that you should go back home before there's any trouble."

"Trouble? Are you insisting that we leave? I told you, we were only sightseeing."

"Germany is not the only country in the world," Egon hissed. "Denmark also has an army. Rifles. Prisons."

The pressure on Egon's arm increased. Egon bit the inside of his mouth to keep from crying out.

"Who is *that*?"

Instantly the focus was on Egon.

"This is my friend." Sergeant Thompson squeezed Egon's arm even tighter. "My *ill-mannered* young friend.

"As chief law-enforcement officer, however, I am both well-mannered and well-informed. And you are neither allowed nor welcome in Denmark. If you'd like, I'd be happy to discuss the matter with you further at our jail house."

"All right. All right." A few minutes, and they'd retreated into the darkness from which they'd come.

Egon massaged his throbbing wrist.

"Young man!" Sergeant Thompson's voice was stern. "That was not very smart." He softened slightly. "They'll be looking for you now, Egon. Not for some young Jewish baker. . . . They'll be looking for *you*."

32

They continued south out of Tinglev. They were alone now, really alone. They walked not slowly, not quickly, but steadily and purposefully.

Egon shuddered to think how close he had come to disaster. His impatience and anger only made his situation worse. Every time.

From now on, no matter what happened, *no matter what happened*, Egon promised himself that he would not snap in anger.

The thought was part of a larger constellation of promises gathering themselves in his mind.

Someday, somehow, he would be more than just a baker.

Someday, somehow, he would go to college.

With each tree they passed, and they passed a great many, Egon repeated his promises to himself. Since anger was his particular problem and controlling it was essential for his survival, Egon repeated that promise twice as often as the others.

Finally Sergeant Thompson spoke.

"As I told you, my orders are to take you back to Germany. And I've always been a man who obeyed orders."

Egon barely noticed that Sergeant Thompson was smiling.

Smiling.

The sergeant spoke again. "See that star?"

Egon nodded dumbly.

"The next time you come to Denmark, stay two fingers to the right of that star and you won't get caught." He held up two fingers in demonstration.

Egon stared with disbelief.

"Do you understand me?"

"Yes, sir."

"This section of the frontier is less traveled. My patrol won't cross this area for at least another four hours." They kept walking. "But of course, you do have to go back to Germany."

"Of course. . . ." Egon paused. "Thank you." Imagine, thanking the man for taking him back to Germany. But they both knew that wasn't the reason.

The forest was very different this way, denser and darker, without even a hint of a path. The sergeant stopped again and again, giving directions, making sure Egon understood how to avoid getting caught. And each time they stopped, Sergeant Thompson repeated the official line: "Of course, you have to go back to Germany."

Egon wanted to hug the man. Tomorrow was as uncertain as ever . . . but tonight he was being shown a compassion he could never have expected.

Egon could no longer see Sergeant Thompson's face, but he could feel the man's goodwill.

"We have a large and stable Jewish community in Copenhagen. I understand the synagogue is quite beautiful. Pity you have to go back to Germany so soon. Perhaps on your next visit to Denmark."

"Yes, perhaps." Even here, deep in the woods, they kept to their roles.

For the first time in days Egon felt a genuine optimism, even hope. Soon his mother would receive the letter telling of his safe escape.

It would be nice, of course, if things were more certain, if he could be sure of exactly how everything was going to work out. But life was far too complicated to have any expectation of a neat and tidy end.

Yet, no matter how black the world became, there were people willing to reach out. He had seen proof—in the Nazi innkeeper, in the compassionate Thompsons. Often it was very well camouflaged, but there was clearly an inherent goodwill that transcended politics and religion. He had seen it. He was seeing it right now.

Sergeant Thompson stopped near a small clearing.

The moon and the stars reflected against the white snow in the clearing, illuminating both the stiffness of his official coat and the warmth and genuineness of his face.

The two of them just stood there for several moments. They had nothing in common but the present. It was, however, such a powerful present that each, for his own reasons, was in no particular hurry to let it go.

"Well, I told them I'd take you back to the border."

Egon looked around at the moss-covered trees. The snow, the pine needles—all of it looked exactly like those they had walked over. Never had it been so clear that a line of demarcation was arbitrary and ephemeral.

"This is the border?"

Sergeant Thompson nodded. "You remember what I told you?"

"Yes, sir."

Just to be sure, Sergeant Thompson repeated his directions.

"I've done my duty." They shook hands. "Farewell."

"Thank you."

The sergeant turned to leave. As he did so, Egon moved to follow. The older man shook his head, but with a smile. "At least wait until I'm gone."

And so he did.

As he stood there, alone, forcing himself to wait, Egon realized that he didn't even know the man's first name. The man knew his, but names weren't really important.

As he walked forward into his new country and his new life, Egon felt quite firm in his absolute understanding of what was important.

He was alive and he was free.

Afterword

Although I have taken some liberties in the telling, the basic story of my father-in-law's scooter accident and his increasingly desperate attempts to escape Nazi Germany is entirely true.

There at the deserted section of the German border where Sergeant Thompson left him on Christmas Eve 1938, Egon set his sights on Copenhagen. Slowly and carefully he made his way toward the city he hoped would be a safe haven. He spent one night in a chicken coop doing deep knee bends to keep from freezing to death. He was once mistaken for a Nazi. Several times he was almost shot.

Three months later, in March 1939, he made his way alone to Shanghai, where he was later joined by Bruno and one sister, Cecilie. In China during the war, Egon managed a bakery and became known in the Jewish refugee community for ''Katz's bread.'' He spent all his money in futile efforts to help his mother and sisters who had remained behind. For two years Julie and his sister Gertrud sent ever more desperate letters to China. One card, from Gertrud, stated cryptically that her husband was ''already not here,'' as close as she could safely come to saying that he had been deported.

In 1941 the letters stopped.

It's only recently that we have learned some details of what happened to those who remained in Germany. In 1937, a year and a half before this story takes place, Leni was taken by the authorities, assigned a number—496—and forced to work as a domestic in a nearby town that was a collection center for Jews who were being deported.

Gertrud and Leni were both deported to the east in 1941. Whether they died of illness or were killed in one of the various camps is not known, since Nazi record keeping with respect to Jews was scanty, euphemistic, and often inaccurate. Their ultimate fate, however, is a certainty.

Julie Gruenewald Katz never gave up the hope of reuniting her children and refused even to consider leaving Germany herself as long as Leni's whereabouts were unknown. For a while Julie lived—alone with her candle of hope—in her house in Barntrup, a small town near Hanover in northern Germany. Later, as officials consolidated the few elderly Jews in the region, Julie's sister and another aged couple were ordered to move in with her. Like all remaining German Jews, after September 1, 1941, they were forced to wear a yellow Star of David on their clothing.

Julie Katz was almost seventy-one years old on July 29, 1942, when the storm troopers came. From a nearby collection area she was sent to Theresienstadt. The cousins I call Sam and Berta, who ultimately survived, saw her in that labor camp. We are not sure whether it was weeks or months later, but witnesses also placed Julie and her sister on the train to Auschwitz. Survivors agree that upon arrival in the death camp, elderly people were separated from the group and never seen again.

Egon's niece, Susan, was eight years old when she was sent to England as part of *KinderTransport*, a church-sponsored program to save Jewish children. Later she emigrated to South Africa, where she lives with her grown children and grandchildren.

Bruno is now a retired teacher living in Hawaii.

After the war Egon served for a time as a ship's baker in the merchant marines. Ultimately he came to the United States and was able to fulfill his mother's dream, and his own, of pursuing a higher education. He became a citizen of the United States at the first opportunity and changed his given name to Eugene. After he was married and the father of two sons, he became a certified public accountant.

For many years Eugene Katz had his own accounting firm in northern California. He is retired now, and travels to Europe often. Painful as it is, he always returns to his hometown.

The house that he grew up in is much changed. The gleaming gourmet butcher shop, with a home above, is typical of the new, modern Barntrup. Along with a few small factories, the town also boasts a tanning salon and, of course, a video store.

The small Jewish cemetery is not neglected, but it is definitely an anachronism. There are no Jewish people living in this entire region of Germany.

Eugene goes to city hall for the key to the cemetery.

The stone is black. Tendrils of ivy grow around it but do not obscure the inscriptions. Max Katz is buried here. Eugene had Julie's name added later. Many years have passed, but he has never forgotten her soft gray eyes, or her tears—or what happened to his family, and to so many others.